THE PASSENGERS YOU CANNOT SEE

The Behrg

Cover by Mat Yan. Editing by Karl Drinkwater.

ISBN-13: 9798610030142

TABLE OF CONTENTS

ALSO BY THE BEHRG

Housebroken: A home invasion horror novel where the kidnappers offer no motive; want no ransom. They are here only *to observe.*

Happiness is a Commodity: A dystopian novella of a future where Happiness must be be purchased from the government. And the price is going up.

The Creation Series: An apocalyptic thriller series where the seven day process of The Creation has begun anew in the jungles of the Amazon. But in order to Create, one must first Destroy. Begin the series for free by signing up for Behrg's Newsletter at his site: thebehrg.com

DEDICATION

To all those traveling dark paths.
Even if they don't know it.
Yet.

*"After all this suffering, the faces seemed to ask,
are we to accept that suffering is the point?"*
— Dennis Lehane, *Since We Fell*

DRIVEN

They will call her Monster. Child killer. A seething psychopath. Though right now she is just another hapless driver fighting traffic on her daily commute, unaware of the destination to which she will arrive. For her next stop is not a location, but an act, each road sign leading to the same place. The same word.

Murder is not a location to which one drives, rather it is a location to which one is driven. And yet the destination beyond this act will ensure the woman lives forever. After all, straight is the road, and narrow the gate. But watch closely. Read carefully. For within this tale, the secret of eternal life will be revealed.

Though seemingly ordinary, the difference between this woman and you or me are the passengers she's picked up along her way, the ones you cannot see. The ones silently goading her to crank the wheel, slam her foot on the gas, and smash her car into the center divider. The ones hoping she'll drag more sacks of flesh and bones with her as she cruises toward the circular drain easily mistaken as a tunnel entrance. The ones driving her to her destination like a jockey whipping a steed, even though she is the only one behind the wheel.

At the age of six, she picked up her first passenger. Mom had gone through a carousel of boy toys, men of different ages and sizes, each entering one car door and, after a few miles, departing through another. Occasionally they'd leave behind a memento, grease stains on the seats or smudges on the windows. A spot of vomit on the carpet that gelatinized into a hardened mass. But though Bill Sturges left her mother and their lives after fourteen months—a longer courtship than usual for her mother—he never got out of the vehicle. He became a fixture, a part of the car's interior. A festering wound that, whether picked at or not, never healed.

He shattered the girl's arm with a toaster. Not just a break; in the x-ray her bones looked like a window pane that's had a rock thrown through it. But she quickly learned his outbursts and sudden fits of rage were her fault, not his. Because she interrupted him during a game. Because she laughed too hard and too loud. Because she was too stupid to know what was good for her. Because her momma was a good lay, but good lays came with fine print, and she was the excess baggage. Because, if he ever had a daughter, he hoped to God she'd be brighter than her.

The arm healed, though it still aches in the winter, and the feeling in her thumb and forefinger are just this side of numb, but despite her mother moving on to other men, the girl never moved on. Not fully. Bill's large hands remain forever on her shoulders, turning her about; his voice a constant echo in her ear, a reminder that it's her fault.

It's always her fault.

Teachers and friends, bullies and neighbors—all occupied space in her car, coming and going, though never staying. They'd leave behind food wrappers or smudges on the windows, torn seat cushions and an array of graffiti—scribbled, spray-painted, even carved into the overhead cloth and upholstery. Every one of them tried to have some permanence in her life, branding a mark they hoped would remain, unaware that in so doing they became just like all the others, for trash blends in best with other trash.

The next permanent passenger was one she hoped would never leave. Seventeen, and in love. It was a storybook moment. It didn't matter that Devin Cook was ten years her senior, or that he traveled for work, or that he'd sometimes not get back to her for days at a time, setting her world spinning like a top at the edge of a high-rise building. It didn't matter, because he always caught her in time. Kept that top from coming to a complete stop, or from sailing over that edge into the oblivion beyond.

They built a future together, constructing it one bucket of sand at a time, until their castle became a village—a city—with towers that went so high they blotted out the sun. At least until the tide came in.

Wave after wave beat against what they had built, dashing walls and towers, cityscapes and elaborate tunnels; waves that couldn't be stopped. For Devin Cook already had a family. A wife. Kids. Two cats.

A mortgage. A neighbor boy he paid to mow the lawn every other week. Their life together was the fantasy, and soon Devin Cook disappeared beneath the undertow without even raising a hand to wave goodbye. Without reaching out for her to save him, which she would have—despite having watched their castle erode into just another common bed of sand. She would have. Because she loved him.

It's been years since that beach was laid flat, but no matter how many times she's taken her vehicle to be detailed and cleaned, there's always sand in the crevices of her seats. It grinds in the seatbelt lock, preventing the latch from fully clicking in. It puffs up from the floor mats, and blows fine grains out from every air vent. She's gotten so used to the sand being a part of her life that she expects the meals she eats on the go to have that granular crunch, swallowing it down with the bile that threatens to rise every time she thinks of what could have been. The castles no one will ever know of.

Other lovers have entered and exited her car, though she makes less frequent stops these days and is far less likely to unlock her doors. One brief encounter, a stranger whose name the woman can't even recall, provided the unfortunate seed that spawned the next permanent passenger in her vehicle. One that required a car seat.

In a movie montage, the car seat coming straight out of the box would gently begin to show its age, with discolored stains and plastered crumbs appearing. It would then be swapped for a high-back booster that would similarly age, followed by a booster with no back until, at last, only the regular seatbelt would begin to show frayed edges and signs of use.

But in the woman's vehicle, the car seat was never replaced.

It still resides in the backseat, a relic that has aged only from time, not use. The plastic edges are cracked, its fabric and designs long faded, but there are no crumbs. No stains. Only a dangling mobile that occasionally spins with a hard turn. And yet that presence, and its angelic or demonic cry—take your pick—can never be silenced. Not even when the rain pounds against the roof and windows of the car. Not even with the radio turned up as loud as the cheap tinny speakers will go. Not even when the woman screams herself hoarse, trying to hear her own voice over that repetitive wail that knows no consolation, that will not be stopped, for ghosts—real ghosts—are louder than thought. And far more determined.

Other passengers include a boss who exacted much more than an eight-hour shift out of the woman, and a psychiatrist who got off on coaxing her patients into overdose and suicide (and who is now serving time, while concurrently occupying a seat in the woman's car). There's even a supermarket teller who would follow the woman around the store anytime she entered, just to make sure she didn't steal anything. The vehicle is crowded, filled with competing voices that prevent the woman from thinking for herself, or at least hearing the thoughts she might otherwise have.

And so, as the tunnel approaches, the woman does what any sane person might when pitted against an army of conflicting viewpoints and belligerent backseat drivers. Ones that can't keep their hands from scraping against the wheel. Though there's a tunnel ahead, the woman knows from experience there will be no exit. No light announcing an end. This tunnel leads only to further darkness.

Somewhere behind her, Bill Sturges reminds her it's her fault.

A quick calculation; a single turn of the wheel. The car seizes, intending to continue its forward momentum despite the unexpected change in direction—though really this is the direction the woman's been heading all her life.

Like the chamber of a revolver, the world begins to turn. For a moment while airborne the other passengers are silent, surprised by the woman's sudden initiative and determination. Or perhaps they're contemplating the end result of their actions, and just whose end such a result will include. For in driving the woman towards her final stop, the collateral damage will stretch beyond the dozens of vehicles that will pile up in what will be known as the most horrific traffic accident to occur on Interstate 40. For with the woman's life, their own lives will also be extinguished.

But our story does not end here, with the death of a single woman. Hauntings rarely do. Besides, this story has always been about achieving eternal life.

With the woman's death, she moves from one vehicle to many. Though she no longer sits behind the wheel, she travels down hundreds of roads, accompanying those drivers who cannot forget. Those that lost loved ones in the crash. That lost the use of their legs, or watched as their own elaborate sand castles were laid to waste by an unforeseen tide. Their lives have been permanently altered by the passenger who has taken up residence in their cars, the one reminding them that nothing is safe. That tragedy will strike without reason. That once its icy fingers are around their throats, it won't ever let go.

The passengers you cannot see. We each have them, driving as we are down our own unfettered highways. And yet how many other vehicles have we inhabited, our whisperings and secret thoughts guiding those drivers towards an early exit? One that doesn't end with more road ahead. We, too, can help those drivers live beyond their mortal lives, spreading throughout the cars of those with whom they come in contact. For the goal, if not a happy ending, has always been to live forever. At least in someone's mind.

ONE STAR

"This will be the last blog entry here at Modern Maiden of Horror."

Li pauses from typing and considers how best to approach her post. Opening paragraphs can turn a reader off as quickly as a 3am infomercial. And yet what spews out of her head and onto the page in the next few moments could very well determine her future. And whether that future will include time spent in a state prison.

She continues:

"I do not write today to clear my conscience or defend myself, nor am I looking for a showing of support. A man is dead—a life cut short —and there is no right or wrong in this equation. But in an effort to dissuade rumors from taking hold, I will lay out the facts as clearly as I am able, all the while mourning the tragic loss of an individual who was as real as you and me, with hopes and dreams and—yes, even fears."

Plenty of fears.

Li highlights everything after "all the while mourning," replacing it with: "over the terrible tragedy that has taken place."

She rereads the paragraph in its entirety.

Better.

Her screen's brightness drops several degrees, preparing for hibernation. Within the darker display, an image moves just beyond the words, a reflection that isn't quite her own. It raises a metallic object into view as it lowers its head, preventing the gun from being fully seen—at least from the vantage point of the display.

Words float over the image like raindrops against a window pane.

Li slams her laptop closed. She knows what comes next. She's seen it a few hundred times—even after every social media site pulled the video down. After all of her book blogging friends called, texted, or DMed in an uproarious panic. Even after the first call from authorities came in.

She's not sure it's something she'll ever stop watching.

She raises her laptop screen, casting off any reflection with the screen's renewed light. At least for the moment.

She types:

"At precisely 2:52 yesterday afternoon, William Han, who writes horror and genre fiction under the name Jaxon Creed, committed suicide while on a Facebook live stream. He claimed my one star review of his latest work, *Lost Roll of Film*, was, if not the reason, at least the catalyst that led to his final act. After much contemplation, I have chosen not to remove the review of this novel from my site as, either way you look at it, the review is now a form of evidence."

Li highlights "the review of this novel," adding a hyperlink to last week's post: *THE ROLL OF FILM ISN'T THE ONLY THING LOST—A #BOOKREVIEW OF JAXON CREED'S LATEST BLUNDER*. Not that anyone in the book blogging community hasn't read her review, at this point. She even has a message on her phone from Vanity Fair who's gotten wind of the story and would like her comments on a piece they're preparing. Probably some biased critique that goes beyond the landscape of publishing, calling into question whether every Dick, Jane, and Joe who believe their voice should be heard really deserve a platform—even if it is one they've created for themselves.

Outside her one bedroom apartment, a car backfires. The noise is so similar to the gunshot on the video that Li minimizes her screen, pulling up the recorded video to watch it one more time. Han's hand rising as he lowers his face. The audio signal clipping with the boom of the gunshot. William Han dropping out of frame. The back of his head remaining in focus as his forehead presumably crashes onto his keyboard.

For the next thirteen minutes and twenty-two seconds, there is absolutely no movement on the video, other than the slow shifting of splattered goop over the laptop's built-in camera, specs of bone, brain, and tissue creating a kaleidoscopic view. A person who is breathing—even one attempting to minimize any errant movements caused from such an act—will almost inevitably display some sign of life.

Li would know. She's tried.

She pulls her post back up. Between the transference of one window to another, the brief reflection she catches on screen looks far more like William Han than herself.

She writes:

"It is not my place to determine whether my review crossed a line. While critical of Han's novel, I made it a point—as I do with every review I write—not to attack the author, but rather to focus on the points of his story that did or didn't work for me. In this case, there was much that didn't. That's not to say the story wouldn't work for other readers. I've discovered novels that I've enjoyed immensely based on another blogger's critical review. Reading is a subjective experience, one we each bring our own backstory into, which inexplicably changes the words written into a narrative that can only be experienced once. It's as close to real magic as anything we could possibly achieve, for how else could the same letters and words put into the same order create such a vast and varied experience? Even if you reread the same novel, the days or weeks or years that have passed will have changed the way you interpret things, spinning a story that, while similar to what you remember, will still be at least partially new.

"This is the beauty of reading and writing, a secret to the universe that we are all privy to. It's why I've never shied away from sharing my honest opinions. Han's previous novel—or Jaxon Creed's, if you're into pseudonyms—was a book I couldn't put down. *Brick by Brick* was wicked fun, and you can read my review here."

Again, Li pauses to link the text to her review, written almost a year ago. It was one of the first reviews on her site.

She continues:

"In writing this post I am not trying to defend myself. I own the review I wrote for *Lost Roll of Film* just as I own the tragedy such a review might have incited. Like William Han, and like many of you, I'm acquainted with mental illness and the drain it can be on both body and mind. Turning words meant to be constructive into an attack from which relief can't be found. Deep down I know my review isn't what caused William Han to take his life, but I can still mourn my decision to upload my review in the precise moment where Han was at a tipping point and needed only one more thing to send him tumbling over that edge."

Taking a moment to reread everything from the top, Li runs a hand through her short hair, styled like a boy's. Her mom would've hated her new haircut, though in truth there's little of Li's life her mother would have found acceptable. Some people will never understand the demands required of those married to the arts. The need to create. But not only to create; to have one's creations brought to life.

Li pushes back from the tile counter and stands. The kitchen is tiny, the standard-sized fridge preventing the dishwasher across from it from fully lowering. Two of the three overhead lights are burned out, one from well over a year ago. Over a matter of time the adjustment to less light in her life has become the norm.

A silver magnet on the fridge with a raised half-mask, purchased at a showing of Phantom of the Opera in Las Vegas what seems like a lifetime ago, casts back the reflection of a face that isn't her own. William Han, his spiky black hair and chubby cheeks, stares back with a morose expression.

Masks within masks; stories within stories.

"Don't look to me," she says, opening the fridge and pulling out a bottle of Coors Light from behind the half-empty milk carton and styrofoam container of yesterday's left-overs.

When the fridge door settles back into place, it's not Han's face the barrel of the gun is pressing into in the reflection of the magnet, but Li's. She doesn't flinch when her reflection's head turns downward seconds before the gunshot goes off. Gore splatters against the refrigerator door. Li wets a rag at the sink without trying to analyze what just occurred. The psychosomatic residue doesn't wipe away with ease.

One of her first creative writing instructors in college spent almost half a semester pounding into her students the advice of William Faulkner, to "kill your darlings." She claimed every writer holds onto elements in their stories that are solely for them. Identifying and eliminating those "darlings"—while difficult—was what separated amateur from artiste. Li's certain, however, that none of the students in that class would have ever thought to take such a concept literally.

She scrapes the bottle cap of her beer against the underside of the counter's edge, letting the bent cap fall to the ground, then sits back in her chair at the counter. The beer she sets beside her laptop, untouched. Her screen is dark again, but this time there's no reflection staring back at her—not even her own.

You can't haunt what's already dead.

Or maybe it's—*You can't haunt the one doing the haunting.*

Even her thoughts are open to revision.

She presses the power button, the screen's glow filling the room. With each cursor blink a gunshot sounds in her mind.

One darling down, one still to go.

This is always the hardest part.

She writes:

"I became a book blogger because of my love for the written word. While I've dabbled at fiction writing myself, I don't have the discipline nor the drive to do what these talented authors do. I truly admire every one of you, whether I've had good things to say about your books or bad. As an admirer, this blog has been a way for me to feel a part of that process. I hope that in the end, the good intentions I have had will be remembered more than the darkness I may have unintentionally caused."

The final bulb in the ceiling goes out, swallowing the room in darkness other than the light from her screen. Or at least that's how it would happen if Li was a character in her own story.

She continues:

"As I said at the beginning, this post isn't a call for help. I have looked at my life and found myself condemned, and I refuse to allow this darkness within me to affect another struggling soul. While I will save you from having to witness my end, the guilt of what my actions have caused is more than I can bare.

"I have surreptitiously decided to join Han in an early exit from this life. In many ways this world was always too bright for a creature of the night like myself. My only hope is that, should there be something in that great darkness hereafter, I will be able to find Han and encourage him to keep sharing his visions in the world beyond.

"Thank you for accepting me into your community, however briefly, and never let someone else silence your voice. Until you discover at least, as I have, that you must silence your own.

"Farewell from your Modern Maiden of Horror."

Rather than go back through her post, revising sentence structure and word choice, Li clicks the button to publish now. She doesn't bother adding keywords or hashtags, knowing the post will go viral in a matter of minutes.

While Li has never written "The End" upon completing a novel or story of her own, she has a ritual which must be followed. She chugs down the cold beer, tears running down her heavy cheeks, then smashes the bottle against the tile countertop. This is the only time she ever drinks, having lost her mother to a drunk driver, but death requires a dulling of the senses. Even if that death is for a friend others might consider "imaginary."

Few people understand the intimacy of creation. Of seeing the world through someone else's eyes—their dreams, their longings, their suffering. Yet as each story arrives to its natural conclusion, that connection is inevitably severed.

Every novel results in death. The deaths of every character within the story—including those who survive. For regardless of whether there's a happy ending, or a denouement with promise of more to come, the character's lives—their stories—come to an end.

Tonight's death, however, feels even more real. And while Li knows this is just another character she's created, a dark part of her psyche wonders if we aren't all just imaginary, playing the role others have written for us. The part in their story they demand we fulfill.

There's a reason Li doesn't drink more often.

Her computer screen still has some of the dried muck from Han's suicide plastered against it. She taps the keypad, the dark screen coming back to life in a way her characters never can.

Closing out of her Wordpress platform, she logs into Amazon's publishing portal and scrolls through the dozen pseudonyms she writes under. Li clicks on Jaxon Creed's name, then allows the site to refresh. She smiles. The sales from the beginning of the month are eclipsed by the insane spike that occurred with Han's death. And they've only grown stronger in the week since. Sure, she had to cut her hair and become—for a moment, at least—a boy, but this just felt like the natural progression for Li's writing, inhabiting the lives of her characters not just on the page, but in the real world. Making them as real to others as they've always been to her.

Now, adding the double suicide of the blogging persona Li created a year ago to help bolster her own work with positive reviews, she expects sales will not only remain strong, but put her into the category of best-seller. As in *New York Times* best-seller. There will be repercussions for the way she's achieved her success, but in the end her creations will not only be out there, they'll be brought to life by millions rather than the few dozen readers who accidentally stumble onto her work.

To think, the stratosphere of success hinged not on her work being well thought of, but on a one-star review. And a story that would captivate an audience, whether they realized it was written or not.

Li lets the screen turn black, her word-count done for the day.

Standing behind her in the screen's reflection is not just the fictional Han, but every character she's ever written, in every story she's ever inhabited. Their ghosts are with her always, filling her apartment. Her world. Her life.

But these aren't ghosts she's afraid of. After all, she is the one haunting them.

EVERY HOUSE IS HAUNTED

This house is haunted.

Cindy knows it—she's *always* known it—even if her boyfriend Barry and their mutual friends think she's out of her mind. It never bothers them when they enter a room and find the furniture rearranged, or when the most commonplace of items suddenly disappear, vanishing into the ether. They've dismissed writing on the walls even when it remains there, a permanent reminder of the supernatural. Their apathy to the hauntings taking place have almost caused Cindy to question her own sanity, until finally today she realized the truth.

It isn't the house that's the problem. It's her friends. Regan and Tina, Jack, and even Barry—they're the ones haunting her.

She's not sure when it began, and in truth she and her boyfriend have been together so long, details of her pre-Barry existence are hazy, at best. Their friends play such an intricate part of their day-to-day lives, they might as well be unknowing victims of a TV series, with strangers watching their interactions and chuckling along to a pre-recorded laugh track.

Only lately there hasn't been much to laugh at. Sure, Jack is still a klutz and Regan has different colored hair every time she comes over, but their conversations have fallen into trivialities and clichés. It's gotten so bad Cindy often wonders if they aren't just repeating the same conversations, tape wearing thin from being constantly replayed.

But her suspicions have turned from a wispy idea, nagging like that tickle in the back of a throat, into the full on confirmation of runny nose and sneezing fits, with a dry cough you can't shake. For one, she's never been to any of her friends' homes. They only ever visit her. Sure, maybe they'll all go out for a picnic, or even spend a day lounging at the pool, but they've never invited her to their place; never reciprocated her and Barry's hospitality. Of course it's hard for a ghost to have you over, except in the home they're actually haunting.

The other thing Cindy should have picked up on, and yet for some reason never has, is how often they're around. Don't they work or have lives other than to keep her company? And while they talk about their jobs, it's always in generalities—Tina bragging about her salon; Regan talking about the dog or cat's life she saved for the day (even though she looks nothing like a veterinarian, and certainly doesn't work the hours such a profession should require); Jack going on about "being in the office," as if that's the extent of the knowledge he has regarding what he supposedly does for a living.

And then there's Barry. The man she's been planning to marry for as long as Cindy can remember. Oddly, he's gone a lot more than the others, and when he's home there are certain expectations Cindy is required to meet. Keeping the house tidy. Having a fresh cooked meal ready and warm the minute he gets home. Bringing him a soda when he's watching the game, or massaging his feet before bed. These aren't things that bother Cindy, though they might most women, and Barry certainly feels real enough to her. They even kiss every night when he gets home from work. But the fact that he refuses to acknowledge everything that's wrong with the house has Cindy suspecting that he's one of them, or at least in cahoots with the others.

Despite all of the crazy happenings—the posters appearing on walls that no one purchased or hung; the dinner chairs breaking, then miraculously reappearing fixed; the flowers in their garden never dying, despite no one watering them—Cindy could convince herself that she's happy. Even settle in to this existence, as imperfect as it might be. But Barry refusing to believe her? Or worse, questioning her sanity as if all of these things are normal? Well, Cindy might not be an expert on relationships, but she's sure there should be a little more trust involved than that.

Which is why she's decided to move out.

Today.

Right now.

It might not be permanent; in fact, she hopes Barry will seek her out. Beg her to come back, or move in with her at the new digs. If he's not a ghost himself, of course.

There's no time for a moving van, nor would she want to give any of her supposed friends a reason to suspect her betrayal, but there are a few items she needs. A change of clothes. Her favorite hand mirror and comb. The locket with her and Barry's picture in it.

The flight of stairs are narrow and set at an unreasonable incline, and though Cindy dreads even the thought of making her way to the second floor she knows she has no choice. She waddles back and forth on her feet, looking like some demented penguin, as she makes her way up, wondering if this will be the last time she sees her home.

There's no bannister or rise at the landing, the stairs inset directly into a bedroom. A big screen TV against the wall and treadmill in the center of the room, this is where she and Barry work out together. Maintaining the figure Cindy has isn't as easy as some people would like to believe.

She moves to the open doorway leading to the Jack-and-Jill bathroom, which is between the work-out room and her and Barry's bedroom, when a voice causes her to stop.

"Hey, Cindy, whatcha up to?"

She swallows hard, knowing Jack wasn't in the room when she came up the stairs. But in the hanging mirror next to the doorway she can see him on the treadmill, sitting languidly rather than actually using the dang thing.

"Just looking for my comb," Cindy says. She's always had a tough time telling a lie.

"Oh, you mean this one?"

She turns around to find Jack now standing on the treadmill, her comb sticking out of his outstretched hand. His smile is alarming, plastered on his face as if he's hiding a secret. And then, without any movement of his own, the comb rises out of his hand, floating in the air until it passes through his hair, before returning to his grip.

"Thought I'd get a work out in after a long day at the office," he says. "Welcome to join."

They know I know.

The thought is crippling, but Cindy isn't ready to give up yet. She nods, backing into the wall, then scoots to the doorway. "Have you seen Regan or Tina?"

"Oh, I'm sure they're around somewhere." Jack's smile never leaves his face.

"Keep the comb," Cindy says, then backs into the bathroom.

A large tub takes up half of the space, a toilet along the far wall next to a counter and mirror. There's so little privacy in this home, Cindy wonders how she's survived as long as she has.

She moves toward the doorway to the master bedroom, when Tina appears directly before her in the tub. Not only is she fully clothed, she's also sitting *on top of* the water rather than in it.

"Hey, girl," Tina says, as if everything's normal.

"Please . . . don't hurt me."

"What are you talking about?" Tina suddenly stands on the water, then leaps out of the tub, landing next to the counter, completely dry. "Oh, this," she says, picking up a hair dryer. "You're right, we totally shouldn't keep this by the tub. Might cause an accident. But you've had a long day, why don't you get in?"

Regan stands next to Tina, despite never having entered the room. Her hair today is a burnt orange. "Baths are the best way to relax, Cindy. Even the pets at my clinic know that."

They move as one, forcing Cindy back until her legs hit into the tub.

Tina waves the hair dryer in her direction. "I could always blow dry your hair *while* you're in the bath. Save some time?"

Cindy glances around for something to fight them off with, but comes up empty handed. There aren't even any bath towels or bottles of shampoo she can throw at them. "Leave me alone!" she shouts.

"No one wants to be alone," Regan says. "Even the little dog I saved today—"

Cindy interrupts Regan, shoving her way between her friends. "I've heard enough of your stories!" She half expects to pass right through them, but instead is forced to jostle her way through, their bodies as real as her own.

Tina drops the hair dryer, which rattles on the floor. "Ow, Cindy, what's gotten into you?"

"I just—I need to be alone!"

Cindy rushes through the open doorway into the master bedroom. Furniture is sparse, with a bed that takes up most of the room, a single wardrobe set against the wall. The ceiling slopes downward with the awkward cut of the roof, the far window accessible only while crouching or kneeling. But it's the bed that holds Cindy's attention. The bed, and who is sitting on it.

Barry is propped up against the headboard, the locket Cindy came to retrieve held tightly in his hands. She should never have come for it.

Either Tina and Regan are standing silently behind her or they've vanished, as ghosts are wont to do. But Cindy knows how this game is played, and this scene was only ever meant for two.

"Were you really gonna leave?" Barry asks.

The hurt in his voice is so readily apparent Cindy wants to rush over and tell him everything's fine, that they can be together forever.

"Without even . . . saying goodbye?" His head swivels towards her and she struggles to meet his gaze.

"Everything's wrong here," she says.

Barry slides to his feet and tosses the pillow and blankets aside, overturning the bed in the process. "I do everything for you, Cindy— everything—to try and make our home the perfect paradise, and this is how you repay me?"

He pulls open the doors to the wardrobe, tossing her clothes to the ground and trampling on them. "Nothing's ever good enough for you, is it? Including me!"

"It's not you I'm trying to run away from, Barry. It's this house!"

The walls begin to vibrate, the single chandelier above the bed bobbing like the end of a fishing line.

"Do you feel that?" Cindy asks. "The earthquake?"

Barry looks at her with deadpan eyes. "You're sick, Cindy. Up here." He points to his head.

The room continues to shake, a screech sounding, followed by three claw marks appearing along the wall. The gouges are deep and long, created by a hand much larger than Barry or Cindy's heads.

Cindy says, "We're going to die if we stay here."

Another scraping noise—this time four marks are raked along the floor, pulling up the wooden tiles.

"Maybe we're already dead," Barry says.

The chandelier slams against the ceiling as if struck by some unseen force, then falls to the ground, shattering against the overturned bed. Something heavy pounds against the wall next to Cindy, a hole breaking open. It allows a view inside the bathroom, where both Tina and Regan sit on the floor, their legs outstretched in front of them. Neither of them move.

"We could have had it all," Barry says. "Lovely home, beautiful life. Maybe even kids were in our future?"

The screeching returns, sounding like a car crash, and Cindy isn't surprised when half of the back wall is ripped open, right next to the heart that mysteriously appeared on the wall with both Barry and Cindy's initials in it. A heart neither of them drew.

"Nothing here is real," she says.

Barry tosses the locket onto the ground in front of her. "Am I not real?"

"I won't let you haunt me anymore."

"Cindy, Cindy, Cindy," Barry says. "We were made to be haunted."

Cindy snatches the locket from the ground, the only thing she'll bring with her from this terrible place. Voices come from the doorway behind her, all three of her friends begging her to stay.

"Don't go!"

"We're so happy here!"

"This home is all we need!"

She braces herself, then rushes toward the far window. Barry doesn't even try to stop her. "You can check out anytime you like," he says, letting the clause dangle, but Cindy knows this one. Her mother loves The Eagles.

Only Cindy does leave. As the house continues to tear itself apart, wood splinters flying in the air and fresh holes appearing in the ceiling and floors and walls, Cindy throws the window open, ducking to crawl through. The drop is far, but her legs are long, and when she hits, she rolls, preventing any serious damage. She takes the jeep out from the carport and keeps from looking in the rearview mirror as she leaves her old home—and life—behind.

The new house is gorgeous, easily twice the size of her previous home, with three stories instead of two, but it's the silence Cindy finds the most rewarding. No neighbors popping in, telling her about their day. No boyfriend demanding she keep the house to perfection. She even leaves the dishes out after her meal, with plans to clean them instead in the morning. She'll have to pick up some new clothes, but even that will be therapeutic. Like most women she knows, Cindy loves to shop.

She considers drawing a bath to relax, but decides instead to go to bed. It's been a long day. She kicks off her shoes and collapses onto the mattress, not bothering to remove her skirt or top. That's when she sees the writing on the wall.

It wasn't there the first time she walked through the house. Wasn't even there when she entered the room. Scrawled on the wallpaper, just above the nightstand, are the letters C & B, with a red heart drawn around them.

Cindy traces the outline of the heart, identical to the one inscribed on the wall at their old place. As she sits back down on the bed, she gasps—sitting atop her nightstand, the one she was just leaning over, is her comb.

"This can't be happening."

The door to the wardrobe across from her slams shut. The end of her dark blue gown—*the color of midnight*, Barry always called it—sticks out from between the crack.

Voices reverberate, crawling through the thin walls all the way from downstairs.

"Cindy, we're ho-ome!"

"This place is amazing—I bet we'll even have our own rooms!"

"Hey, Cindy, what gives? You ate without us?"

Cindy rests her head in her hands, a sense of inevitability sweeping over her. There's nowhere to escape. Every house is haunted.

As Barry and her friends appear in the room—not one of them entering through the doorway—Cindy prepares for what might be her last moments alive. But then a voice shatters her every thought, so loud and strong it might as well be the voice of God.

"I'M PLAYING! WHAT? NO, WITH THE NEW DOLLHOUSE!"

Cindy watches as Barry and her friends fall lifeless to the floor.

The voice returns, shaking every loose piece of furniture in the room. "FINE—I'M COMING!"

And then Cindy is dropping to the floor, her limbs going limp. She's unable to catch herself as her head smacks against a bedpost, followed by the wooden floor. A few inches away, Barry's unblinking eyes stare into hers. Though his lips never move, his debonair smile impeccably in place, she hears his voice—whether in her head or spoken out loud, it no longer matters.

"I tried to tell you, Cindy. Tried to warn you—to help you see. This is what we were made for."

But Cindy refuses to give up. Life is more than the thin plastic shelling you're born into; the role others want you to play. Just because she was made for something doesn't mean she can't break that mold. Become something more than anyone intended.

She concentrates—trying to stand, to force herself up, to move of her own volition—and yet her limbs remain inanimate. She can't even close her eyes to better focus. Still, she continues, hellbent to at least get away from Barry's unnerving stare. And then . . . her foot rises, leg lifting ever so slightly on its own. Her arm bends, awkwardly at first, but enough to put her hand in front of her and push up off the ground.

Her head swivels, taking in the sight of what she's never before seen. Where a wall should be, her house opens into a room that dwarfs her tiny home. A room within a house that is not her own.

Cindy's lips turn downward, relaxing the smile that's been forced upon her. She knows what role she is to play, albeit on a bigger stage; a larger house. After all, Barry and her friends taught her well. If gods have homes, they too deserve to be haunted. Every house. Every home. And Cindy has plenty of material to draw from.

The smile that flashes across her face is one that will soon give a little girl nightmares.

THE TROPHY THIEF

5:48 am.

A faded red truck pulls to the curb on Devon Street, towing a white enclosed trailer still dripping from a recent wash. It is the only vehicle parked on the curb in this neighborhood. On the back of the trailer, the words "Do-Gooder Landscape" accompany a forgettable logo and Jesus fish placard. No phone number or website on the trailer; the fish, according to the Owner, is good for business.

The Owner and sole employee of Do-Gooder, Inc. steps out of the truck holding a coffee from a bloated franchise. Steam rises from the slitted lid, but the Owner doesn't sip from the cup, he takes a long pull. Then another.

A worn straw hat with frays splitting between weaves is pulled low upon his head, his dark blue jumpsuit—almost the color of night—speckled with stains like fading stars. Thick calloused boots and leather gloves complete the uniform, though they lack the tie-dyed tinges of dying greenery one might expect of a gardener. Even the speckles, upon closer inspection, aren't ember but a shadowy molten red.

5:52 am.

The Owner leaves the driver's door open as he moves toward the rear of the trailer. He wishes he had a cigarette, though he abandoned that habit over twelve years ago. As a man of principle he admits only one addiction into his life, and if he can only choose one, there's no question which it will be.

He removes the padlock and opens the swing out doors to the trailer, the Jesus fish disappearing as if darting beneath a reef. He doesn't pull down the ramp. Not yet. That will come later. Instead he leaves his coffee somewhere in the layered depths and removes a simple cordless weed-eater. It's one of his favorite tools—light, quick to load, yet loud enough to compliment the illusion, allowing him to disappear behind the white noise of ordinary life.

5:56 am.

With a chortle the weed-eater starts up, buzzing viciously as it inhales the overgrown weeds and grass of the Rosenberg's yard. Dirt and rocks are spit out like broken teeth as the tool is brought near the trunk of a tree. The grass and weeds may be left uneven, but the Owner is not concerned. No one examines the background of a painting from a distance. Neighbors complaining from the early-hour noise are also not a problem; the Rosenberg's home foreclosed months ago, and no one has touched the yard since. Concerned neighbors will forgive the annoyance and plunder back to their beds, assuming the bank has finally hired someone to do something about the place.

An assumption that will be wrong.

5:59 am.

Above the noise of the weed-eater, the Owner hears the door of the house directly across from the Rosenberg's open. He doesn't know how he hears it, but he does, its whooshing sound like a lover catching her breath. A calculating invitation.

The Owner wants to look, wants to throw down the stupid gardening tool and stare at the man exiting his home, his castle, oblivious to the realm he so arrogantly will leave undefended. In lesser times, a foolish tyrant like this deserved to have his kingdom taken. The Owner forces himself to turn away from the house he knows so well. He is part of the scenery, just another dog barking or car driving past. By now he knows this one's routine so well he can almost see the man bending at the waist to grasp his toes in an awkward stretch.

The man across the street is a runner. The Owner loves runners, especially disciplined ones. In some ways he finds them similar to himself—dedicated to an absurd cause, yet men of principle. Their discipline makes his job easy.

This morning the Runner will go through exactly seven minutes of stretching on his porch. The Owner's not sure why the Runner doesn't stretch inside the warmth of his home. He suspects that, like so many of the Runner's supposed status, everything the man does is only real if others see him doing it. At least in the Runner's mind. Seven minutes of stretching, a minute-and-a-half putting on, tying, and retying the shoes, and then a six mile run in forty-two to forty-four minutes.

More than enough time to do some good.

6:02 am.

The weed-eater chokes out its last chwonk and unexpectedly dies. The lack of noise is a problem. It makes The Owner vulnerable. Makes him visible. He has inadvertently stepped into the foreground.

Across the street, the Runner hops on one leg pulling his other foot back. He wears a beanie to cover his baldness and his shoes match his running jacket—bright yellow. This one always color coordinates. And then it happens—forced into the foreground, the Runner returns the Owner's stare. He has noticed the Owner.

Most in this scenario would incorrectly break eye contact, finding a task to busy themselves with in an attempt to create doubt. Like spotting a cop when speeding, the natural reaction is to slam on the brakes and try to blend in. The problem is the space between shifting gears—what is meant to hide only magnifies, replacing doubt with certainty. The correct response is to simply do the unexpected.

The Owner does so by continuing to stare at the Runner, his chin brought to rest on his hands as he leans against the busted weed-eater. He allows himself to float into a memory so distant, it seems of another life; so cherished, it feels like only yesterday. He no longer looks at the Runner, but through him, at the past. The acquisition of his first trophy.

The Owner was eleven and he wasn't an owner yet. The only thing he owned was the reputation of being worthless, like the gardening junk he would later acquire at yard-sales. The peeling rubber on his shoes had more value than his contribution to life, and this according to his beloved mother. He learned at an early age to blend into the background, becoming just another fixture in the remnant of their broken home. It was the only way to avoid the collision that would undoubtedly occur from his coked-up mother or her bad-news boyfriends. While the faces of those men would change, their interactions with the young owner were always the same.

He hated them all. His mother, for rewarding those soulless drones with the attention he could never earn; and the men, for accepting such a gift with the slipperiest of intentions. He sought a way to prove to his mother he would never be like them, that he was better than them all.

At school a science fair project was announced, a competition where the top contenders would not only earn recognition, but be presented with trophies—tall pillared towers of gold ensconced glory. It was what he had been waiting for, his way to finally stand out.

Each day he would pass the other school kids riding their bikes in driveways or playing hoops in the street, as he walked past their manicured homes and fell upon the dirt road that lead to his dilapidated farmhouse. The others could play all they wanted, he was dedicating himself to a cause. He was principled, and he intended on winning that competition.

His project was based on a loose hypothesis that a human brain worked similar to a camera. As vision focused on a subject, prioritizing it over its surroundings, the peripheral objects became less important. Unfocused.

His experiment involved several tests where he placed before subjects (mainly his mother's boyfriends) three images he had drawn to great detail. The first had a naked woman in the center. In the background was a farmhouse with a farm boy branding a cow, and a faceless farmer stabbing hay with a pitchfork while holding a baby.

The second image had another naked woman in the center, though this time the farm boy pressed the steaming brand against the crying baby, and the farmer without a face stabbed the pitchfork into the cow.

The third image had the farm boy front and center with the farmer stabbing the pitchfork into the naked woman and the cow giving birth to the crying baby. He let his subjects inspect each image for three seconds before removing it and replacing it with the next. At the end of the experiment, he asked them to repeat what they remembered from each image.

It came as little shock that his hypothesis had been correct. In the first two images, the subjects only talked about the naked women, remembering vaguely the farmhouse and people in the background. Not one of the subjects remembered what those people had been doing.

The third image's results, however, were less than satisfactory. All but one subject didn't remember a farm boy, instead placing the young yet-to-be-owner in the picture. They thought it a self-portrait. And though the farm boy had just been standing there, two-thirds of the subjects remembered him killing someone or something—the cow, the naked woman, the farmer; in one instance, a goat; in another, himself.

Nearly every test he conducted ended with a beating, his subjects becoming so livid they would lash out, calling him demented, perverted, insane. Black eyes, broken ribs, and split lips were common during those days—such was the cost of science. Eventually he began to imagine he was the farm boy and the depictions of death leaping from his mind became more real than the shadowed landscape of the barn he crept around the edges of. What the young artist failed to realize was how his project was about to become a second experiment in itself.

Up to this point, he had managed to remain under the radar in school, an unfocused face always present, never remembered. His experiment changed all that, bringing to the foreground behavior ignored for years. Due to the graphic nature of the pictures presented, he was immediately suspended from school.

As trophies and ribbons were handed out to the top projects, the young Owner watched through a side window to the auditorium, balancing on top of the trashcan that held his months of labor. He recognized the trophy winners as the same boys and girls he had passed in the streets each day. They hadn't conducted their experiments or built their projects, their parents had. And yet there they stood, glowing in the praise and applause of their peers, the school teachers, and the other parents. Accepting what they had not earned.

That day the young owner waited outside the school yard, returning to the background he now realized was home. When his classmates emerged carrying their prizes, their fake golden statues hefted upon shoulders, he fell in with their number as they walked home. One by one the children separated from the group, each drifting to the castles they called home, until the young owner was alone with the girl who had taken first place.

She had passed her house long ago, but, as she had told the group—not the owner—she wanted to show her trophy to her grandma, who lived only a few blocks down.

They walked together, leaving the pavement in exchange for the dirt country road. Neither of them said a word until the young owner kicked a rock in the middle of the road. It skipped across the dirt with puffs of dust striking, leaving a small dent in an abandoned Volkswagen.

The girl inhaled sharply. "I didn't realize you were there."

The young Owner smiled. He knew not a single one of her friends would remember him accompanying them that day. His smile grew as he envisioned them talking tomorrow. The police reports would be out by then, and they'd wonder what evil had befallen this sweet poor girl on the way to her grandmother's.

He left her body in the side of a ditch, leaving her exposed pale flesh for the flies to feast upon. Her trophy he took with him.

The next morning, the trophy had been moved to the mantle in their living room. His mother never mentioned it, but each trophy he brought home joined the first and he knew, in her own way, his mother was proud.

6:08 am.

The Owner emerges from his memory as if waking from a long dream—disoriented, unsure of his surroundings. His hands slide from the weed-eater and he almost falls to the ground, a tree offering its support to keep him aright.

He glances around, then across the street at the Runner who has been watching from afar. The Owner waves, casting a look of embarrassment and shaking his head as he scoops to pick up the fallen tool. The Runner nods, smiling and returning the wave with a shake of two fingers. He puts on his shoes, unaware of the Owner returning to the background.

The Owner shrugs into his invisibility like a familiar coat. It emboldens him—he stands, no longer daydreaming, but staring down the man who will so soon give up his most prized possession. The Runner, of course, does not notice.

The trophies have changed over the years. The Owner no longer craves the fake golden statues that so enamored him in his youth. These days, fake golden hair tops the trophies he now collects, stealing away the prize less-than-worthy men have never truly earned.

Today's trophy is a perfect statuesque figure that could only be shaped by a surgeon with skill or a god filled with lust. Her golden crown will be a spectacular addition to his already robust collection.

6:12 am.

Returning the weed-eater to the dark nothingness that is the trailer, the Owner watches as the Runner places buds to ears, hits a button on his enslaving watch, and flees from his castle. It's almost too easy.

The Owner closes the trailer and moves back to the cab of the truck, its door still open. He watches through the windshield as the Runner disappears from view, rounding a corner that begins the six mile loop he runs every Wednesday.

The door to the castle will be unlocked. The Owner knows because he's checked. On several occasions. Like most runners, this one prefers not having the distraction of jangling keys to disrupt the fluidity of his workout, instead trusting the machine that keeps repeating its soothing pattern that life and people are generally good. The Owner's fingers drum against the steering wheel.

He begins the countdown.

Three minutes. He read somewhere about the human brain's response time to prescient warnings. Humanity long ago mastered the ability to ignore the promptings most would describe as coming from their gut. Inklings; internal red flags; those thoughts that something doesn't feel quite right. Far easier to rationalize such thoughts away than contemplate how wicked the world can truly be. The article or journal he had read considered three minutes to be the breaking point, at which time—if the warning bells weren't heeded—there was almost a zero percent chance of responding to that initial concern.

Until, of course, the consequence of ignoring it came about. To this, there would always be a response.

And so the Owner adopted the principle of allowing his victims three minutes to change their mind, to respond to the threat that so callously hung over them. Three minutes for a runner to turn back.

No runner ever has.

6:13 am.

With two minutes remaining, the owner closes the truck's door. He is anxious, and with the trophy within grasp he decides a change in procedure is due. He doesn't owe the runner three minutes, he wants the trophy now.

He backs the trailer into the Runner's long stone-colored driveway and hops out, keeping the engine running. In a matter of seconds the trailer doors are open and the ramp extended, kissing the edge of the garage. He touches the garage doors and can almost feel the warmth of his trophy waiting inside—it reminds him of the warmth of a blazing farmhouse sent up with barrels of gasoline, where a naked woman was found dead with a charcoaled baby and cow. Police reported that the man's body found with them had his face removed prior to the fire.

The Owner grabs his tools—his real tools—against the inside of the trailer wall. A thick rope, knotted into an adjustable figure eight, a black burlap sack, and a long machete with curved blade and polished handle. The rest of his tools wouldn't be needed until the trophy was brought home for display.

6:14 am.

One minute remains, but the Owner has already forgotten the Runner. He brushes against the side of the trailer door as he moves onto the porch of the castle that houses his trophy, for by now it already belongs to him.

He turns the doorknob. It is unlocked.

Time to do some good.

He lets himself in.

As the trailer door swings back and forth ever so lightly with the breeze, the Jesus fish appears to be swimming, lolling side to side with the motion. If it could open its mouth, it would show layers upon layers of twisted fangs—not a Jesus fish, but a Jesus piranha.

Twenty seconds remain and the street is empty. Quiet.

Fifteen seconds.

Twelve.

Ten.

In the distance, the echo of a faint noise is heard. A slapping sound, of weight being thrown around. A rhythmic muffled pounding.

The Owner has begun his work.

Or maybe, just maybe, it's the slapping of feet responding to a feeling that can't be shaken, that something doesn't feel quite right.

KILL YOUR DARLINGS

Carl Renkins couldn't outrun the kind of day he was having.

The heat of the afternoon sun glared up from the paved road, matching the temper of his thoughts. Ordinarily, the chaotic and yet somehow rhythmic balance of feet pounding, music blaring, and heart thrumming, combined with the short inhalations through the nostrils and loud exhalations through the mouth, would send Carl into the Zone—that void where thoughts simply cease to exist. But today even the Zone avoided him.

His creative writing instructor, Ms. Bartlett—all two-hundred-and-eighty pounds of her—had handed back his first assignment earlier today at the Community U. It was the only course he was taking—partly because it was all he could afford, but it was also the only course he needed. Even the word 'need' was a bit of a stretch. Carl would be a writer, a famous fiction author specializing in horror stories of the macabre that would make your grandmother's hair turn white. If it wasn't already. He had decided long ago to apply in his studies the advice a famous author—he couldn't recall the name—had once offered to would-be-writers: skip the boring parts.

Carl was hoping to gain from his class *the* answer that would propel his writing from "tinkering with a hobby" straight to the best-seller's list. It was a secret every self-respecting real author knew, yet never revealed. They hinted at it, sure, in writer's conventions and self-help articles that were really mocking writers like Carl; inviting them to a feast (*"Come on in, help yourselves…"*) where all the food was made of wispy dreams and unfulfilled desires. Where you could fill your plate with helpings of Character, Plot, Theme and a side of Point-of-View, and still walk away abased and famished. Where A-listers making their millions used the heads of writers like Carl to rest their filthy feet upon as they laughed, gallivanting in their circle with other famous writers, at all the amateurs come to lick up the scraps of every syllable they vomited out.

It was only a matter of time. Enough classes, enough research, and Carl would prove he was worthy of the secret, and just like that overpriced video of the same name promised, the doors to the universe would open themselves to him.

Their first assignment had been an open submission, a short story of 3,500 words or less. No subject or prompt, the teacher had wanted to get a feel for each of the students' voice and style. One afternoon Carl had banged out a piece he was particularly proud of about a homeless man—Gil the Grille—who followed and then murdered the people who refused to give to him. The dramatic irony in the ending he especially loved, as Gil donated the organs of those he killed to research, so in their deaths they finally became charitable.

There was no breeze, but Carl felt goose bumps on his arm. That ending was killer.

His story had been handed back with one letter in red at the top, the letter that began with the word Carl had immediately uttered. Not a single note of correction in the entire piece until the very end. In a hurried, barely legible scrawl, the message—*"Write what you know."*

Carl pushed up a hill, imagining the road was a springboard like the fleshy rolls of his teacher, and each pound of his foot was him kicking common sense into her obfuscated skull. *Write what you know.* He should've listened to the adage "those who can't, teach."

What was she looking for anyway? A depressing memoir of a twenty-something teen with grandiose dreams about writing who had no idea where to start? Throw in a dead-beat father and overly paranoid mother as support characters and—*ta-da!*—a sure-fire recipe for a bestseller! Where do I get in line for that? Or how about the tale of a fast-food worker who's obsessive compulsive girlfriend had, mid-orgasm—(his, not hers)—went off like a child with Turret's, dumping his ass as he tried to make it all last one second longer. The sex, the girlfriend, the feeling of having something in his life to make it worth living.

The Zone had avoided him that day as well.

Carl knew a lot about not keeping a job, about begging mom and dad—now that Kathy was out of the picture—for money to scrape by on rent. Video games, late night TV, and how to grocery shop for a week on a budget of twenty dollars summed up his life experience. The whole point of writing was to get away from what he knew. He was bored with his own life, why the hell would someone else want to want to read about it?

He rounded the corner that would slim his eight mile route down to five, then came to a stop. The sidewalk ahead looked like a scene from a disaster movie—concrete pulled up; dirt and rocks littering the walkway; a huge gaping hole in front of a fire hydrant that, until recently it appeared, had been blowing sky high. Water lapped up over the curb, creating a murky, muddy mess. And not an orange cone or bit of cautionary tape to be seen.

Carl hit the STOP button on the phone strapped to his arm, tracking his run. As the ticking seconds came to a life-altering halt, the world around him slowed to an inexplicable pause. It was the Zone, but it also wasn't. It was . . . different, like looking at an image from an entirely new angle and realizing that black vase was actually a picture of two white faces about to get it on.

Carl took a half-step back. The beads of perspiration on his forehead remained in place, floating in the air just before him. Playing through his earbuds, McJagger's careening voice was cut off mid-sentence, jumping Jack never achieving that flash. Even the rippled water with its tiny wave remained still at the curb, peaked at its miniature crest.

An idiot construction worker standing in the hole in the ground was frozen in place, wearing a sweat stained baseball cap rather than a hard hat. Back turned to Carl, he was oblivious of anything other than whatever thoughts floated through a construction worker's empty head while on the job.

A heavy bracketed hose lay on the upturned sidewalk, its tip made of metal.

Heavy metal.

An industrial truck was parked along the street, emergency lights paused in a permanent flash, front door ajar with that RING floating through the air like the distant sound of an ice cream truck— annoying as hell, yet beckoning. Urging Carl on.

Keys still in the ignition, as if Old Sweaty Ball Cap had intended to stop for just a moment and was about to get right . . . back . . . in.

Carl saw all these things from a distance, an outside observer casually watching but not commenting on the scene before him. Like a character in one of his stories, he found himself moving and acting independently of his own volition. He felt the chill that always came from breathing life into something one-dimensional. With fascination he watched as he picked up the end of the hose—that metal tip having a real weight to it, even heavier than he had imagined—and carried it over to the open hole.

Time reinserted itself, leaping forward to catch up—McJagger tripping over his words, sweat dropping to the mud-encrusted concrete, and Carl's shadow consuming the already darkened hole. Loose dirt spilled onto Old Sweaty Ball Cap's sweaty ball cap.

"Rob?" Old Sweaty turned his face into the blunt tip of the hose coming down at a bewildering speed.

Krckkk!

The sound of bones being reshaped.

The hit was softer and quieter than Carl had expected. Old Sweaty's skull hadn't given much of a fight. A dull wrench flew out of his hands as his head crooked into an angle Carl had never seen before. Not on a human, anyway.

Carl leapt into the hole, heart pounding harder than up any incline he had ever run. He brought the metal tip down onto the top of Old Sweaty's head again, like a hammer on an anvil. Or a watermelon, red juice squirting out in a fine mist. Again he was surprised by the sound of the impact—a dampened thud, like it had been surrounded by carpet. Nothing like the movies where every fist fight was accentuated by an earth shattering crunch. The construction worker's body crumpled, head and torso sliding beneath the edges of the hole.

The hose fell from Carl's hands. He felt light headed. Like he was going to vomit.

He reached out, gripping loose rocks and bits of concrete. Tumbling dirt descended like Carl's mind, both settling on Old Sweaty's now bloodstained ball cap.

McJagger's condolences were anything but heartfelt.

Carl ripped the earbuds from his ears but still the music continued. Louder. Stronger. Filling his head—his world—until the drums from the song became his heartbeat; the lyrics, his thoughts; the music, his soul.

His vision went black. His thoughts no longer existed, mind having gone completely blank. He had become, he realized, a blank page, the blinking cursor awaiting whatever would be typed upon it.

All of his worries, concerns, fears . . . like a twisting cyclone of dust, he felt them skittering around at the edges, but when he tried to focus on them it was like looking through a filter of shadows.

He hadn't found the Zone. He *was* the Zone.

A brilliant flash cut through the darkness, expanding Carl's mind and chest as he leapt to that plane where all higher ideas come from. He had felt this kind of elation before, on those rare instances when something brilliant coursed through his fingers as he wrote. In those moments it always felt as if he became the vessel to some otherworldly force, as if the ideas weren't his own but something he had tapped into, channeling some other entity's thoughts. But if he had but sipped at that run-off before, he was now drinking straight from the fountain.

Suddenly he knew—absolutely knew—*this* was the key he had been searching for, the Universe speaking to his soul. This was what his teacher, Ms. Bartlett, had meant with her scathing note. She hadn't wanted him to write some self-pitying novella, she was trying to open his eyes. To the reality of what a novelist—*real* novelist—had to do.

Write what you know.

Every horror story and suspense thriller Carl had ever read flashed through his thoughts like a demonic merry-go-round. Of course! These authors hadn't invented their stories—not completely anyway. No one could articulate such visceral realities without having experienced them firsthand. The sounds and carnal descriptions of murder, rape, torture, and death; that mix of emotions like a seasoned soup—anger, fear, guilt, and most of all power—pure and blinding, coursing through their arms, legs, their fingertips, like electricity preparing to leap from one void to another. These stories were born organically, based on real events, based on . . . what they had come to know.

Carl finally understood what writing really was. The world around him had become his story, to be bent and reshaped according to his will. Nothing could now stop him from becoming the writer he had always dreamt of being.

The slam of the truck door brought him back to his body, back to the hole of his rebirth. Old Sweaty Ball Cap wasn't alone.

"Jimbo? You finish up down there?"

Carl stood erect, watching the heavy set man approach. This must be Rob. Big Rob. A look of dumb shock on his face as his mind connected the fact that Carl was not his pal Jimbo.

"Your buddy collapsed in here. Help me lift him out," Carl said.

"Is he okay?" Rob asked as he hurried as much as a man his size is capable of toward the hole.

Carl picked up the heavy wrench that Jimbo had been using. It felt good in his hands. Right. He would have to remember to describe that feeling, like an extension of himself, not a foreign object or tool. The wrench became just another part of him, and when he swung it up into the face of Big Rob, it felt as natural as pulling his arms back and stretching.

But Big Rob didn't go down as easy as Jimbo, Mr. Old Sweaty Ball Cap.

"Aw, shij man!" Rob scrambled back from the hole, holding his broken jaw in place with his hands. Blood poured from his fingers, running in fine trails down his arms. He backed up against the brick wall separating someone's quiet landscaped front yard from the scene ripped out of a disaster movie before him.

Or maybe it was now a horror flick.

Carl hopped out of the hole feeling lighter than he had in a long time. He picked up the wrench he had set at the lip. Speaking of lips, he didn't see any on Big Rob as the larger man held his hands out to ward Carl away.

"Shjay back!" Big Rob must have seen Carl's smile, because he broke into a run. If you could call it that.

Carl hit the button on his phone to resume his workout as the setting of his story made way for his entrance. Chunks of concrete and rock scattered before him, the sidewalk propelling him forward, assisting his every foot strike like a moving runway. A strong breeze awoke, turning and changing to always be behind him, no matter what direction he ran. Gravity itself lightened its pull on Carl Renkins as he quickly closed the distance. The Universe, it seemed, had taken notice.

He caught Big Rob just after he rounded the corner onto the adjacent street. One swing to the back of his skull was all it took to send Big Rob to a flying fat stop.

Carl felt his heartbeat in every pore of his body. He had never felt this alive. He scooped up the heavyset man by the shoulders and started dragging him back toward the truck when he noticed her. A young mother out for an afternoon jog. Headphone cords reached up to her ears, appearing from beneath her sports bra and drowning out, to her at least, the tired screams of the baby in the jogging stroller.

Their eyes met.

It looked like Carl was going to get in some distance today after all.

***

* * *

Carl's first novel, *Kill Your Darlings*, was an overnight success. About a writer who resorted to murdering the people he knew (starting with his dead-beat father and overly protective mother) in order to write more realistic murder mysteries, it was both critically and commercially acclaimed. In the end, the killer was never caught, leaving potential for sequels.

The movie hit theaters a year later, following the release of Carl's second novel, *The Editor*, about a book editor whose clients would have break out debuts, and then disappear off the radar. One hit wonders. Critics decried the impossibility of someone not taking notice of the disappearances, though Carl felt it was completely plausible. By this time, he had started his own publishing company and had created a platform to help undiscovered talent remove the "un," as Carl liked to say. A few of those writers even had number one best-sellers.

For their first and only novels, anyway.

When asked in interviews or writing conventions about the secret to his success, Carl always had the same answer—he would tell about an inspiring teacher he had studied under. He never gave her name; that would have created problems. Especially when inquiring minds did a little homework and realized Susan Bartlett, former professor at Chapel Community College, had died in the same way as one of the characters in his first novel. A sharpened vacuum hose had been inserted into her chest, sucking up the blood, fat, tissue and eventually life-sustaining organs, a little at a time. A poor man's liposuction. She had remained alive and coherent the first time Carl had been forced to empty the bag-less filter and when the police eventually found her body, she weighed less than a hundred pounds. In some ways, he believed, it was what she would have wanted.

"My instructor, who will remain nameless," said Carl at one of the hundreds of conferences that all blurred into one, "taught me something that changed the way I wrote. Or thought. 'Write what you know,' she said."

The laughter that followed always surprised Carl, despite the fact that it was the same advice as in his novel, the advice that had pushed his protagonist, if you could call him that, into an endless bout of killing. The faceless crowd always thought he was making some intellectual joke. They laughed because they wanted to be intellectuals too. But Carl hoped that at one of those conferences, there would be a struggling young writer who—just like him—would come to realize the full power of that cliché. And that it would awaken in him or her, as it had in Carl, the ability to become a real writer.

To become a god.

After Carl's third novel hit stands, he was more of a celebrity than ever. *Afterword*, about a writer who hid details of real people he had killed in the afterwords of his novels (always in praise and thanks) set the world abuzz. Inquiring minds had caught up after all.

Soon on every television and internet newsroom Carl Renkins' face was displayed along catch phrases like: *Writer's Success Founded not on Craft but Crimes*, and, *Horror Fiction Writer's Life More Barbarous Than his Works*, or Carl's personal favorite: *Renkins Releases Autobiography . . . In the Novels You've Already Read.*

Through the trial Carl remained calm, composed even. He testified of what he had done, and why he had done it. He held nothing back. What would have been the point? It was all there in his books.

In between court dates he signed contracts for exclusive interviews, movie and book options, but not about *Afterword*, or his characters. It was *his* story they wanted, *his* life, though in truth, Carl often thought of himself as one of his characters. Just another fictional creation.

After the sentencing, but before Carl was incarcerated, he met with Barbara Walters in an interview as one of the most fascinating people of the year. It was quickly decided by all parties involved, Walters included, that Carl would make the top of that list, a decision later vehemently opposed by various right-wing groups, yet held to by the network. They later celebrated their decision. Ratings were the highest the network had ever seen.

The interview was short, mostly because Carl wanted it that way. But at the end, Barbara asked him the question he had been hoping for, the reason he had agreed to the interview in the first place. When the shit hit the fan, so to speak—not Barbara's wording, but Carl understood the question all the same—why hadn't he run? Why hadn't he gone underground or skipped out of the country? Why leave so many clues that were bound to be noticed, if not now, eventually? Had he secretly wanted to be caught, as so many profilers claim about serial killers? What was going through his head? America wanted to know.

Carl's answer was not what she had been expecting. In fact, it surprised all but those few Renkins disciples who had studied his work, his interviews, and begun to apply his teachings to their own budding craft.

"I always wanted to write a story about a prison escape."

PATTERNS

I woke to pounding at my door, and not the neighborly—*I'm so stoned I thought this was my place*—sort of intrusion. This was the insistent knocking capable only of those in a position of authority. I honestly don't know why they knock, it's not like I keep locks on my door. An inquisition at this hour could mean only one thing:

They had found another body.

In the past two months this would bring the count to four, an absurdly short time for that many deaths in this neck of the woods, where most residents live to the ripe old age of needing a nurse to wipe their butt. The fact that all four deaths were suicides—or at least I presumed this new one would follow a similar M.O.—was another checkmark in the category of "odd and disturbing findings." It was far from the only entry in that mysteriously queer box, but more on that later.

I'm not sure if I let them in, or whether they tired of waiting and eventually entered on their own, but they quickly confirmed my suspicions. Another life lost. Tragically taken. This one by hanging.

I'd like to say I was surprised by the face in the photo—and I could have been; in death, no one looks like they do when breathing and alive. But even with the dissimilarities, I knew. It was her.

Tiffany.

If I'm being honest—and let's face it, why else would I be writing this if that wasn't my intent?—I knew it was her with the first knock on my door. I knew it was her four days prior to her suicide. The Authorities, as they like to be called, weren't in the habit of hounding just anyone when a body turned up. No, I had earned an esteemed place on their speed-dial.

Lucky me.

They knew of my talents, my . . . abilities. Sure, I might call them by another name, one that begins with the letter C and rhymes with *nurse*, but it was all I had ever known. And my readings were never wrong.

I see patterns. Not the lines and squares in a wavy piece of fabric, or the caste of symbols etched in ancient tombs. I don't have extraordinary mathematical prowess, nor am I able to foresee the rise and fall of stocks, making my cool millions. My ability is much more unpredictable. I can't call upon it at will or even use it to any degree of manipulation, enhancing my livelihood or bettering my circumstances, though Lord knows it wouldn't take much to make things better. But I do see patterns. In people.

The best way I can explain without you physiologically entering my head—(trust me, you'll thank me later)—is to share with you my first meeting with this girl who has now passed beyond our mortal reach. And she was no ordinary girl.

We met at the library, a chance encounter disguised as fate, for fate is something I no longer believe in. I had finished my weekly allotted time without finding anything of interest, and so prepared to leave. Yet on my way out, quite literally, I bumped into this girl who appeared in my path.

To say I'm constantly aware of my surroundings would be an understatement. I'm not good with people, and so try to avoid any and all interactions which aren't institutionally mandated. How this girl not only cleared my subconsciously ticking radar but merged directly into my range, sight unseen, is still beyond my comprehension. And yes, that fate word comes to mind. To anyone's except mine, that is.

She wore a worn denim jacket, the kind that's more for looks than warmth, though the faded elbows, frayed sleeves and missing button brought into question her reasons for wearing it at all. Her brown paper-bag hair was pulled up tightly in a ponytail, square glasses unwieldy on her petite face. Her skin was chalk pale, tree-stump eyes darting like a cornered animal, and not one that might turn back to attack out of desperation but one that would rather lay down and die.

Despite her frail frame and almost specter-like appearance, there was something about her that immediately gripped me. As we collided, loose sheaves of paper and colorful folders dropped from her hands, scattering in the range of a small scale detonation. She threw herself forward for the book that left her arms, snatching it from the air and clutching it tightly to her chest, barely maintaining her footing in the process. *A Storm of Swords* by George R. R. Martin. It would have been cliché in any other library, but here tomes that large were relegated to a single shelf. Considering the wear on the pages beyond her place mark, it was her umpteenth time revisiting that world. While I had never read a fantasy book, I often wondered if I wouldn't fit in those worlds better than in my own.

The first words from her mouth were an extended apology.

"I'm so so sorry."

I might have thought she had a stuttering problem. And when you considered our chance encounter had really been my fault, the apology revealed almost as much as the patterns that immediately swirled around her.

I became lost, momentarily seized by the shifting paradigms. It's difficult to describe the patterns I see—the word "pattern" likely leading you to a conclusion that's deceptively wrong. I don't see shapes or repetitious markings, it's more a bending of the fabric of space; a warp that enables me to see into the past, the future, into the center of a person, understanding them better than they could ever know themselves. I know how crazy it sounds, but when you consider the patterns I've seen have never been wrong—not once—well, you start believing them without questioning why or how.

As I drifted into the essence of what made up this young woman I found that she was an outcast. Abandoned by her family, her only friends existed on the pages of the books she read. She was the type of girl who would fall into the world of a story so completely that daily tasks like eating or sleeping would ebb away like the lazy hours passed at a river's edge. The type of girl who donned her glasses not for clarity but the worlds that would reveal themselves to her. She had discovered the secret to youth, to living ten-thousand lives within her lifetime, becoming the kings and queens, space travelers and magicians, thieves and monsters of the worlds she entered.

"It's my fault," I said, in a rare moment of clarity. I bent down, trying to help gather the unbound pages that had scattered across the floor—the cost of keeping the worn world in her hands from following a similar fate.

She snatched them from me, stuffing them beneath each other, caring less for their order or physical state than ensuring I hadn't the chance to read what they contained. I found myself intrigued, an emotion almost as foreign as fear.

Or love.

She glanced at me for the briefest of seconds. So why did it feel like an eternity? In those uncertain eyes I saw the truth of who she was. Her pattern again opened itself to me and I knew . . .

"You're writing a book."

Her face fell, cheeks blossoming red. She pushed the glasses back onto the bridge of her nose as she folded the pages and stuffed them into the hardbound Martin novel.

"And it's good. So good you're afraid to continue."

Now she really looked at me. Not a glance. The patterns swirling around her head were exquisite, some of the most intricate I'd ever seen. In them I watched her writing, every minute of her day not spent with pen to paper still engaged in the constructing of her universe. In them I read her book. It was nothing short of a masterpiece. A book that would turn the fantasy world on its head, opening the door to a new level of creation. Nothing would ever be as genuinely ingenious, created in such simplicity, innocence and perfect form. She was a goddess, spinning the fabric of life and lives into an intricate web of such varied beauty it was impossible not to believe in a greater something, for surely an impassioned soul like this could not have been born of the soup and slop of DNA without divinity alighting upon her.

Tiffany. I suddenly knew her name and had no need to ask it. I also learned her work would not only change the world of fantasy writing, but give hope and light to generations to come.

And then her pattern turned, becoming a dark smudge. A shadow spread across it like an eclipse overtaking a savannah. Encompassing all. I suddenly knew. This attractive yet vulnerable girl who had constructed such defenses she no longer realized how far removed she was from the world; this girl that I found myself drawn to in a way I had never been before, not in a "oh, I want to get into her pants" way, more an "I want to get into her head;" this poor girl—her pattern declared it so, and so I knew it would be—would commit suicide within the week.

Now, you're probably wondering why I didn't tell her—*I couldn't*— or why I didn't stop her—*I tried*. Oh, how I tried. Seeing the future doesn't mean I know the intricate steps that lead to that predetermined eventuality.

I couldn't, of course, make our meeting known to the Authorities lest I become a subject of interest myself. But the fact that so many had fallen to a similar fate made me wonder if they had only been staged to look like suicide.

I decided right then and there I had to save her. Had to try.

"Who are you?" she asked.

"Danny. Like the . . ." I had to catch myself, had been about to say, like the Trail-Ridger's nephew in her book. "Like the song. Danny Boy." That was the best I could come up with? "My friends call me Denny. My mother was British." I shrugged, hoping (and failing) to hear her concede through laughter that she found me somewhat clever.

"I'm Tiffany."

I know.

"It's nice to meet you, Tiffany." I didn't extend my hand. I found the reading of patterns only grew mottled once physical contact was made, colors and shapes blending into a collage I could no longer understand. If I was going to save her life, I needed every unearthly advantage I could draw upon.

Tiffany waved the papers buried in Martin's novel before my face. "How did you know? I mean it could be a project, classwork; anything?"

But you don't go to class.

"It's hard to explain," I said. "Tiffany, can I . . ." I paused, suddenly aware of my physical state, remembering why I didn't approach attractive women not only more often, but at all. "I . . . I'm sorry."

Her eyes lost their glimmer as she moved from within the spotlight to the background of the stage of life. She nodded, then moved past me, darting through a cluster of bodies who ignored her, except for the occasional jostle given as she passed.

I cried out, "Tiffany, wait!"

She paused, had been waiting for me to say just that. Whatever words I was supposed to say after never came. I've never been good with words. At least when vocalized. But even without reading my pattern somehow she understood. We left the library together.

The next three days we were inseparable. Mornings I would find her or she would find me. Meals would pass; sometimes we'd eat, other times not. Lights out was like pulling lovers apart at a concentration camp. And in my bed I would lay, unable to sleep, Tiffany lingering in my mind like the pleasant smell of honey-wheat bread fresh out of the oven. Our conversations were elevated to that plane few ever reach, where ideas communicate unbound, unchained, free to move and grow and leap and soar. A conference of the minds. Her pattern flooded me so completely that I found myself spilling over, and—not for the first time—sharing a glimpse of the pattern with its owner. Sharing with her who she really was.

As she at first glimpsed partially and then more fully partook of her potential, the awkward shy girl she once had been disappeared before her true brilliance. She shone so brightly I found myself unable to look at her for long periods of time. And still I kept my distance, knowing that if we touched the vision would be gone and the darkness return.

In those three days she wrote furiously, allowing the dreams of her mind to escape onto the page. She couldn't stop if she had wanted to, the clarity of her pattern extinguishing all self-doubt. I watched in awe, basking in her light as a fish leaps from the depths of the sea for just a moment in the sun. Every moment was precious.

I will always remember those three days as what they were. Transcendent. The speed at which our relationship grew, as if we had known each other all our lives, was only half of the truth. It seemed our old souls recognized each other from beyond this world, as if we were simply reuniting.

And then it happened.

I'd like to say she caught me by surprise, that I was unaware or unequipped to defend her advances. I'd like to say a lot of things, but truth, I've found, is easier to speak than lies. And when speaking is as difficult as it is for one like me, you end up grateful to spill out the very words that condemn you.

She kissed me.

And I let her.

Just a light peck on the lips, but that kiss held so much more. It held the light of all her penned up desires and yearnings; worlds without end exploded forth from her lips to mine. And as glorious and fulfilling as that moment was, I recognized the poison her lips carried —even as I accepted her love and wished for more, I knew our world would wither away. You see, in my world kisses don't wake the sleeping beauty, it's the other way around. That kiss sealed our fate as surely as continuing to pull a thread that never stops unraveling. And unravel, it did.

I held her that night in my arms. It was wonderful. It needed to be. Tomorrow she would hate me. We talked of plans that would never be, of traveling, having children, of spending our time helping those in need, those who couldn't take care of themselves—as if we had suddenly developed the ability to first take care of ourselves.

She was beautiful that night. I kissed her goodnight.

Kissed her goodbye.

The next day it happened. I slipped.

When I slip, I lose the pattern, or it loses me. It closes itself off, but it's more than that. If you've ever experienced the most amazing sunset, heavenly colors swarming through your brain and opening valves and levers to the inspiration that comes with true reflection— take that feeling and then immediately immerse yourself in the thickest, grimiest cloud of a city bus's exhaust. That's what it's like, but magnify it by an emotional well as deep and vast as the ocean and you'll begin to understand.

Slipping always left me in a particularly foul mood, but I had been there before. It comes with the territory, of what I do, who I am and the reasons behind the why.

Tiffany, however, had never experienced the slip before. And when you're higher than the planets, reorganizing the universe, a slip can be disastrous.

I found her that day sitting on a cold bench staring into the floor. Or through it. Though I sat next to her, she ignored me. George R. R. Martin's book lay open on the bench with her pages trapped beneath— now enough to complete a short novella. I thumbed through them. It was clear she had either dropped them again or, more likely, thrown them. Not that an order could have been enforced.

Each page was filled with the panicked scribblings of an adolescent, violent markings and jittery pen strokes. Nothing more than the imaginations of an unsound and fragmented mind.

I said, "I should have warned you."

"That none of it was real?"

"No, it was real. It's just, what would have been. If you were . . . normal. The patterns, they're just a glimpse. Of what could have been. It never stays. I can't control it."

Whether the silence of what I had wanted to say but failed to made her uncomfortable or she could simply no longer look at me without seeing all that had been taken away, she stood and left. I couldn't blame her, I could only blame myself, for thinking this time it would be different.

The next day I waited for her at every meal. I refused to participate in reading or exploring time, my eyes never leaving the door which led to her hall. By dinner they said if I didn't eat they would have to hook me up to the machines. I told them I was worried about Tiffany. They said they didn't know any Tiffanys. Of course, she would go by a different name here; I should have taken the time to read her name tag. I tried describing her but the words were like bubbles that refused to burst. It took three nurses with sticks to escort me to my room. They tied me to my bed and slipped the needles and tubes into my arm that would keep me alive. I slept, though my mind remained awake, praying into the vast minutes of the night that Tiffany would be okay, that she would forgive me. That she would forgive herself. If a god was listening, he had as much difficulty speaking as I did.

I awoke the next day to that knock at the door.

Tiffany!

My mind leapt, my body struggling to keep pace. But it wasn't her. It was the doctor with the serious face. He covered it with a grey beard to try and hide just how serious it was, but I could always see through the farce.

He approached, holding a clipboard. I knew what would be on the other side. I looked away—I didn't want to see. He waited until I gave in. I always did. Eventually.

He showed a picture of Tiffany. It was recent. Her face, beautiful, though much whiter than normal. Against her neck was a bulging tube, her body lifted from the bed, knees dangling just above the bedsheet, her feet resting against her pillow. She had hung herself with the tubes meant to keep her alive. With her feet touching the top of the bed, she could have saved herself at any time. Proof of her desire to leave this world. I couldn't stop the tears had I wanted to. Her beauty, her greatness, all swallowed by the disease that made her a ghost of what she could have been.

"This is the fourth," the doctor said with his serious voice. "The fourth suicide since you've been under our care. And all four spent a vast amount of time with you in the days leading up to their . . . exit."

It sounded like he had a question, but he didn't know how to ask it any more than I knew how to answer it. Was it my fault? No more than the god that had made these great ones unable to reach their greatness. Or the god that had given me the ability to see what they could have been.

"We're having you moved to a secluded ward. For the safety of the patients."

Some time later a new nurse came in, a woman. Small, petite. She wheeled my bed from the room, my hanging bags of liquid medicine chasing us down the halls like a bad dream. As lights passed over my head in five second intervals, new patterns began forming, playing before my eyes in a haunting display. Beauty and tragedy and the tale of a life left un-lived sprang before my eyes like a slightly distorted reel. As the nurse turned me around, wheeling me into the elevator, the truth of her pattern revealed itself to me.

She would be dead in under forty-eight hours.

As her pattern shifted and bent, the mirrors in the elevator opened up new layers I had never explored—angles to the pattern I had never been privy to from my previous vantage point. Through the reflection, I found myself drawing in the essence of her pattern—its shimmering transcendence finer than a powdery glitter. It spurt from her open pores into the air around her and my every breath consumed it like a devourer of worlds.

I was stealing her soul, draining her life. An unknowing vampire of fulfillment.

She looked down at me, sympathy turning to a smile that never met her eyes. Her eyes that harbored a sadness with a ticking clock of forty-eight hours or less. That's when she touched me, flicking a lock of hair from my eyes. The darkness in the room began to spread.

I'm sorry, I tried to say. She wouldn't have understood had I been able to speak. And what did it matter? I needed her, needed her glow. Besides, lies are a pattern of words I have never been able to speak.

The elevator doors slowly slid closed.

REBORN

In 1974, the Catholic Church sent out a declaration to every bishop, presbyter, and deacon who resided within a sanctioned diocese. This formal document, which you will find (though partially torn) at the end of my tale, has since been repudiated, as have all official communications regarding the Sancto Saepes Motu Proprio. Ask any secretariat of the Church about the rumored incursion and you will receive only shaking heads or drudged denials. You will however find that the mandates held within this clandestine document are stringently, if quietly, upheld to this day.

The following is taken directly from the declaration:

From this day . . . forward . . . no infant child abandoned on or before [a Church-affiliated domicile] shall be admitted within said domicile by a member of the clergy. This sanctioned decree is to be upheld without exception.

My tale, and those unfortunate souls who experienced similar trespasses, will provide more than enough evidence as to why.

It was an April evening in 1971, a day that had been muddled with a constant downpour. It is important to note that this was a time when I still believed in a Higher Power. At twenty-three I was young to have been chosen as chaplain of the Sacred Heart Basilica of the Immaculate Conception. So young, in fact, that I still believed I was doing God's work.

Evenings in Bridgeport, Connecticut were quite dull, and with the hellacious storm our evening services amounted to a dress rehearsal, only vacant pews and the occasional scurrying mouse in attendance— the rain always drove them inside. Sister Bedford, a motherly nun in every sense of the word, had taken to mopping the nave, humming an amalgamation of hymns that no choir would recognize. She was deaf in one ear and tone deaf in the other, but her jovial cheeks and maternal charm warmed the soul (not to mention her chocolate chip cookies, which were divine). I hurriedly gathered the hymnals pew by pew, ready to call it an early night.

There was a chill in the high-ceilinged halls and Father Maggiolini, an old-world coot and the attending Bishop, had gone off to check the pilot of the furnace which was always blowing out. If I recall correctly I believe that rainy season we had a leak in the basement. The water pooling against the outer walls of the church seeped through the porous stones rotted with age. It made for an eerie walk through those long corridors below ground, as if the very walls were weeping.

As we mindlessly went about our evening duties thinking only of the warm wool comforters awaiting our shivering bodies—or at least such were my thoughts—a shocking boom resounded from the outer cloister doors. Sister Bedford dropped her mop, her hands going to her ample, yet covered, bosom. The teetering, towering pile of hymnals which I had collected were sent scattered across the hard marbled floor, pages bristling and book bindings breaking. Who would be out at this hour in such conditions? And why a single knock and nothing more?

My heart seemed to answer the resounding thud with a steady knocking of its own. Please remember, I was but twenty-three, at an age where imagination could still conjure demons from shadows and redemption from a statue of a man on a cross.

Footsteps echoed from the west wing, Sister Nettles appearing, a small candle cradled in her hands. "You're not going to open it?"

Her British accent tugged at the strings of my heart which was no good, considering she had already tied them into a jumbled knot. She was adorable, Sister Nettles—a tiny thing at only five-foot-two. A small crook for a nose, long neck and bony chin and eyes which were much too large for her face, but the disjointedness came together like a tightly woven collage creating something far more magnificent than the sum of the individual parts on their own. While I would not have admitted so back then, I see no harm in doing so now; I was taken by her, and despite my vows there were many nights when she visited me in the lucid realms of sleep.

Before I had a chance to gather my thoughts, Nettles swept past both Sister Bedford and me, cupping her hand around the flame so as not to let it die.

"Allow me!" I shouted, hurrying after her.

She, of course, did.

The ornate iron doors, crested with scenes from the bible so analogous each square could represent your pick of stories, were set in the floor with heavy pins that dropped down, latching them closed. A good eighteen inches in length, the pins required an inordinate amount of effort to free from their catch not only due to their weight but the levers within the flooring that had to be turned just so. Once I wriggled the damnable pin free, I pulled the door open, sliding the pin beneath as a doorstop, as we commonly did at the time.

Heavy rivulets poured down just beyond the alcove of the porch, the night black beyond the stoop. I swallowed hard, noting that no one was there—no gust of wind could have come at the doors with that much alarm, and then Sister Nettles was crouching down, her little bottom pursed out towards me. With reddened cheeks almost as rosy as Nettles', I quickly glanced away. The sound of that sweet Sister cooing brought my attention back, her soft voice answered by a piercing wail.

A baby.

Someone had dropped it at our porch. Like a bag of groceries or an advert for the local theater. And whatever depraved soul left it, had failed to turn it from the stuck position of *ff*—FORTISSIMO.

Nettles motioned for my assistance, gathering up her skirt and glancing out at the darkness. I noticed that despite the lack of a breeze, the candle's flame had blown out. I took in the woven reed basket and infant swimming within a sea of churning pink cloth. Her face was the color of a plum and I marveled at how much anger something so small and innocent could manifest. Oh, if we had only known.

After carrying the bundle inside, I placed it on a raised bench. Sister Bedford crowded in beside me. Her heavy jowls curved her lips downward in a permanent frown though it was apparent she was beaming inside.

"Oh, she's such a sweetheart!" Not surprising—I did mention she was partially deaf.

While Nettles still hovered out on the stoop, Sister Bedford reached down taking the screaming infant, blankets and all, and brought her up to bounce against her . . . well, bouncy chest. "Shh, shh, shh, you are a sweet thing, aren't you?"

"You should wait for the Olfac," Nettles said.

"Huh?"

I knew the name by which Maggiolini was called by the attending nuns, Olfac or Factory, in reference to the persistent body odor which always accompanied the man, redolent of a wet and hirsute dog. It was said that the Archbishop Alcote had once nearly fainted in Maggiolini's presence and, while he had attributed it to his fasting, we all knew the true offender. *'If thy right eye offend thee, pluck it out, and cast it from thee.'* Not so simple with the pungent musk of one's own pores.

Knowing that Sister Bedford was just as habituated with the name, I presumed she just hadn't heard.

"She said you should wait for Father Maggiolini," I said.

"Nonsense. We used to see this sort of thing all the time at the Rectory on Forty-Second—young girls knocked up by married men who should exchange their wedding rings for chains, if you ask me. And besides, a man—even a Father, Sister Nettles—lacks the proper equipment. Now close that door! It's drafty as a turnip field in Poland in here."

"I'll get it." My enthusiasm this time wasn't for aiding Nettles but rather born of sheer desperation to escape the gales of the child's cries.

"Here, here, you sweet thing. Now when they haven't a teat to suckle you can slip them a finger and most times they'll pacify themselves to sleep."

"That's disgusting," Nettles crooned.

"That, my dear Sister, is biology."

I always wondered what Sister Bedford heard next. Whether, for instance, the rending of flesh and snapping of bone and cartilage, melded with the sickeningly frantic slurps and bellicose sucking noises, came to her as something other than what it was. I'm quite certain, however, that she heard her own screaming.

The baby dropped from her arms as Sister Bedford backed away, a smear of gristly red coating its small chin. Somewhere along its descent I realized, it was no longer crying. A stream of blood flowed from Sister Bedford's finger like the curved spray of a drinking fountain. Hysterical and dazed, she tumbled against the back pew, falling onto her considerably padded behind with a loud harrumph.

I braced myself for the thud of the child connecting with the marbled floor but watched with fascination as it adroitly righted itself in the air, landing delicately on outstretched fingers and toes. With the blankets torn off, you could see the rippled muscles in its tiny arms and legs as it held itself in a pushup position. Shoulder blades extended, triceps and deltoids flexed—it was like watching some freak carnival showing off a grown man the size of a baby.

Until I saw its tail.

It slithered out the top of the cloth wrapped around its waist, the appendage ending not in a point but a four tendon knob. The digits gripped the cloth diaper at its posterior and tore it free, twirling it once before casting it aside. Then the tail dropped to the ground, its four tendons spread out like talons, the fleshy knob raised slightly above.

The tail started vibrating. Then the creature was launched into the air.

Sister Bedford, who at this moment was mid-scream, grappled for anything nearby with which to ward off her attacker. Unfortunately we were in a church, not a junkyard or garage or office where miscellaneous items could be quickly requisitioned and repurposed. The hymnals, while scattered on the ground, were several rows up, and all of the wall hangings and architectural ornamentation had been anchored to walls and pillars long ago.

The creature landed between the crux of Sister Bedford's outstretched legs, the skirt of her dress bowing inward and drawing up with its weight. Beyond the tethered muscles which rippled beneath its pale flesh, and of course, the tail, it was difficult not to see a helpless infant propped awkwardly between the nun's quite hairy legs.

"MotherofMercysendthisdemonbacktoitsprisonandblessuswithyour holylight." The words came out in a single gasp and must have struck the infant beast like a psychic blow. It began wailing a piercing and heartrending cry.

"BytheFatherandtheSonandtheHolyGhostIcommandtheetoleavethis holyplaceatonce!"

The creature let out a burp. A chunk of what must have been flesh or maybe a nail dislodged from its mouth, skipping with a wet slap along the floor. The crying immediately stopped. It hadn't been Sister Bedford's words that had caused its panic, just an upset stomach.

The beast's tail shot forward, puncturing a slit in Sister Bedford's dress through which it promptly disappeared. A moment passed in which only our breathing was heard, then Sister's Bedford's eyes tripled in size and she cried out with renewed vigor.

"Get it . . . out of me!" Her legs kicked wildly and she doubled over, a strained consternation coming over her face. "Get it out!"

Whatever paralysis had held Nettles and I bound was lifted, incredulity replaced with a need to act, to save. Though we were accustomed to believing in that which could not be seen, we had little experience with doubting that which was directly before our eyes.

I slid to the floor on my knees, reaching through the slit in the fallen nun's gown, the fabric tearing further beneath my weight. The baby was not on the ground between the Sister's legs as I had hoped. No, the atrocity before me was so unimaginable, so damning to both spirit and body, that I quaked at the sight. As a virgin, this was the first time I had ever seen the workings of a woman. But what should have been a curious fascination was vilified by the sight of two extended feet slithering upward into the cavity of Sister Bedford's vagina, the pronged tail sticking out, pressed deep into the flesh of her inner thigh, leveraging its ascent.

This was not the rebirth I had read of in the Holy Bible.

Sister Bedford's screams by now filled the entire chapel and let me tell you, no choir had ever sung so loud within our humble halls.

Nettles fell against me, frantically clawing at Sister Bedford's dress. "Where is it?"

"It went . . . up," I said. "Where a baby comes out."

Elocution had failed me.

I stood, unable to watch as Nettles plunged her arm in after the creature. I don't remember consciously going back to the open door; perhaps I had wanted to leave, to escape the insanity that had stumbled onto the doorstep of our lives, but instead I shoved that heavy door closed, gripping the metal pin in my hand. The feeling that came over me next was what some might consider revelatory. I felt like a vampire slayer, divinely called to rid the world of evil, armed with only righteousness and a holy wooden cross—or in this case, an eighteen inch bar of ribbed steel.

"No, no, no, no, no!"

Nettles' arm and neck were slathered in blood. She now knelt atop Sister Bedford, pressing both arms against the older woman's torso where a pronounced mound beneath the skin continued climbing northward. The off key screaming had subsided, a milky substance bubbling from Sister Bedford's mouth. I moved back toward the two women, the pin gripped like a miniature baseball bat.

A calm and firm determination had settled over me. I knew what had to be done.

Before I crossed the threshold, Sister Bedford's neck bulged, her jaw dislocating with two distinct mercurial pops. And then, from within her gaping lips and saggy cheeks, the top of a head began to crown. Like a bubble blown from chewing gum, the pink head expanded until, with a sickening suction sound, the creature's full head popped free of Sister Bedford's mouth. The rest of its tiny and slime-covered body wriggled out, slipping down her face to the marbled floor.

The creature leapt off the ground just as I swung the metal pin toward it, my calculated strike instead slashing open the side of Sister Bedford's face from lip to jaw. Another misplaced swing sent fleshy pulp splattering upward, disfiguring the poor motherly Sister even further, though by this point she was quite dead. When the infant scrambled over Sister Bedford's body toward Nettles I acted only as any gallant knight might, but the creature avoided each assault with an uncanny dexterity. Its tail suddenly plunged down against a thick bony knee, vibrating ferociously, then it launched itself at the thin nun weeping over Sister Bedford's body.

Footsteps echoed from the hall, Father Maggiolini's raspy voice lost behind the blood thrumming in my ears. The creature was in Nettles' arms, tangling itself in the tassels of her white smock, trying to scale her. I brought the pin back, leaping forward with my thrust. The chiseled tip of the pin sunk through the creature's flesh as if I had been wielding a sword. It shrieked a piercing cry cut short as the metal rod slid through its small body, puncturing both organs and life.

I exhaled a deep breath, an inner peace coming over me. I had exterminated this foul monster, this infernal beast that had risen from the seventh circle of hell. Then I heard the clatter of a small box of tools dropping to the ground behind me.

"My God, what have you done?"

Father Maggiolini stood at the end of the arched hallway, his eyes giant saucers within murky ponds of wrinkles. His jaw hung open, a puppet no longer in use.

I turned back to Nettles, pulling the pin free from the vile creature in her arms. It slid out with much more difficulty than it had going in, ruptured organs and stringy tissue clinging to the inanimate object. I looked for confirmation on Nettles' face, the corroboration of my innocence, of the true culprit of the massacre we had just witnessed.

Without a word, the child slipped from her hands. It smacked the marbled floor with the heart-wrenching thud I had anticipated earlier, when it had caught itself on fingers and toes. While I could still see the hint of wiry muscles beneath, its taloned appendage had withdrawn, tail somehow retracting into smooth, if wrinkly, skin. The blood leaked from its two gaping wounds in its torso like an overturned jar of ink.

And where the baby once had been, Nettles held a pool of crimson blood cupped within her hands. Dangling from the hole in her gown was the creature's tail. It had speared right through her stomach, ripping into her intestinal track. Liquid feces, mixed with blood, spilled from the puncture wound.

Her legs gave out just as I turned back to Father Maggiolini.

"Look—its tail!"

I never heard him coming. He struck me with the end of a candelabra and I followed my Nettles down.

I was convicted of triple homicide. Life, with no chance of parole. Thanks to our corrupt legal system, and untraceable bribes from the Vatican, a plea of insanity landed me in a more hospitable residence than a federal detention facility. They claimed, of course, that the tail was merely mangled flesh, a part of Nettles' intestines. That I suffered a psychotic relapse, remembering my own abandonment as a child, and was caught up in a schizophrenic hallucination. And the creature —well, dead, it looked as innocent as a newborn. With no biological family to press for an autopsy, it was quietly swept under a very thick Italian rug. What's one cover-up in the history of a Church that is riddled with them?

But I know the truth because I'm not alone. There are others just like me. A nun in Tampa, Florida, who set an infant child on fire; a priest in Tacoma, Washington, who threw a baby from the top of a bell tower; a groundskeeper in Southern Utah, who buried a trowel through an infant's skull.

They've seen what I've seen. They know.

And they're not the only ones.

There's a reason that Motu Proprio was sent out to every church and domicile under the authority of the Pope. And if you don't believe me, ask around. You'll see—they'll all say they don't know why or when the practice of bringing abandoned infants into the church was abolished. But if you look closely while they're giving their answers, you'll notice a bead of sweat trickle down a forehead. Nostrils flaring, when their sinuses were fine before. They will quickly excuse themselves to other matters while apologizing that they couldn't give you more of their time. And then you too will know.

Evil walks amongst us. Or crawls. Cries. Screams.

And we are the ones who must stop it.

AN UGLY RESURRECTION

They were back. Back for one purpose, and one purpose only: they had come to kill me.

Just like last time.

And the time before that.

I remember so little of what befalls me when they are not around. It's as if a wispy grey cloud settles over my existence, snubbing out the day to day. But I remember the murders. I remember the torture. I recall with perfect clarity their greedy eyes and hideous smiles full of missing or crooked teeth, and oh, those chants. I awaken with them ringing through my head. Like a doomsday bell, gonging to greet me, a constant reminder that yes, it can always get worse. My life, my existence, is to be their play-thing, their chew toy, to be tossed around and mutilated at their pleasure and then forgotten until I'm needed again.

Unlike what you may have heard, resurrection is no joyous occasion or cause for celebration. Resurrection is a merry-go-round, whose only exit leads to hell.

Helplessly I watch as they abandon the streets, marching out into the fields in my direction. They even stop to hold hands. Cute, right? But then you've never had your flesh boiled off your bones while they're standing above you, singing. I know they haven't seen me—not yet, at least—but they will. They always do.

The hills are encased in snow and I drop myself into the nearest gully. Hoping. Praying. But Deliverance is a selfish god.

"Gotcha!"

I turn just in time to see mittened claws thrust two pieces of hot coal through my eye sockets.

It's begun.

The surrounding tissue sizzles and burns, pain exploding through my head. I scream in agony, backing away blinded, but more of them are already on me. Something sharp impales the skin below my eyes, breaking my nose and plastering it to my face like putty. They move the spike around, digging deeper, carving out a hollow pocket where my nose should be. Liquid runs down my face, no doubt a combination of blood and the emptying of punctured sinus cavities, and then the spike they've thrust through my face breaks through the back of my skull. The hard shell cracks and gives way, pieces of what must be bone and splintered flesh dropping to the ground behind me.

"No, no, you've gone too far," one of them shouts.

"You're ruining it—use the carrot!" another yells.

"No, here, try this."

Immediately the spike is pulled back out from my face. Swollen tissue clings to it as it's removed, making me feel as if they're not just removing a spike, but my very soul. What replaces it is cool and metallic, like a coin, mashed into the fresh wound. Fists push and pump at the flesh around it, my new deformities treated like children's clay, until it stays in place.

As my eyesight begins to return—much cloudier than before—I feel a noose wrap around my neck and I know my time is short. I've never been hung before. I wonder what it will feel like.

The creatures around me grow anxious, snapping at each other until one voice rises above the rest. "Make him dance!"

"Yeah, a dance!"

"Dance! Dance! Dance!"

The hyped mob mentality grows in volume and intensity.

"Dance! Dance! Dance!"

They always want me to perform. Laugh, play, attempt a handstand. One time they decapitated me, but only after I had recited—of all things—the alphabet song, but backwards. Their warfare isn't all centered around torture and pain. Much of it is psychological.

"Okay, you win. I'll dance." My words are answered with high pitched squeals, as if just the sight of me speaking is cause for excitement. "But I'll only do it up there," I say, motioning to the ridge above the gully. "It will be like a stage."

Their hungry eyes nod in agreement. As vicious as they are, they're surprisingly gullible. My movements are labored, white searing pain streaking through my skull with every shuffle, but I manage to pull myself up to the top of the ridge. I glance back at the road behind me and my mouth drops to the floor. Sure, part of that is the fact that my face is dissolving from a combination of the coals and crude rhinoplasty that was performed, but I'm sure shock has at least something to do with it. Deliverance, it seems, has finally heard my cries.

Blue and red lights spill from the top of a police cruiser, which has pulled behind a white sedan out on the road. Someone's bad day may just prove to be my salvation.

The creatures begin their chanting anew. "Dance! Dance! Dance!" But there will be no performance today.

"Catch me if you can, you bastards!" I bound off toward the road and my awaiting rescue.

The town square is pregnant with noise, cars honking and brakes shrieking and pedestrians deliberately ignoring one another. Behind me I hear the monsters approach, screaming with undulated delight. It's all a game to them. My life—my death—all jolly, happy fun.

Tearing over the hills of snow, I burst out onto the road. Cars swerve and I hear the unmistakeable noise of a crash, but I don't bother looking back. All I can do is move forward.

And hope. And pray.

The officer catches sight of me. Whether it's my horribly disfigured face or the pack of creatures at my heels, he drops his clipboard in alarm.

"Please, help!"

I've never been this close to breaking free from this eternal cycle of death. But instead of helping, the policeman unholsters his firearm and yells, "Stop!"

The world around me tilts. I see it all as if I were peering down into a swirling snow globe, my mind leaping with each development, each jigsawed piece snapping in place with a frenzied finality. Children screaming, onlookers gaping, the wind snagging the handkerchief strung around my frozen neck. A woman drops a shopping bag on the opposite sidewalk, hands moving to her mouth. The policeman— young and inexperienced, now that I can see him more clearly— throws his hands in the air as if to shield himself, forgetting about the gun in his hand. The car isn't braking fast enough.

Also, it's snowing.

I brace myself for another gruesome death, wondering how far my body will fly? What my brains will look like, strewn across the pavement like wet crinkled confetti? How long it will take them to scrape my remains off the slick asphalt?

When the car finally strikes me, I find I'm not propelled through the air but rather pulverized. My body breaks apart as if the very atoms holding it together suddenly decide they've had enough. I guess I know how they feel. My upper chest and head remain in place, riding on the hood of the engine for the last few feet before we finally come to a stop. The poor policeman, I think he may have wet himself.

The creatures rush the car, unaware of how close they came to joining me on my trip. Just seeing them approach, my heart picks up its pace. At least this time I wasn't melted down.

They claw and scratch at the car, until one of them wins out over the others, climbing up onto the vehicle beside me. "See you soon, Frosty," he says, reaching for the hat atop my head.

I close my eyes, knowing that when I awake, I'll be surrounded by them again. Brought back from the dead for one more trip down memory lane. A road paved with unanswered pleas and rejected prayers and enough deaths that the road should be renamed 'Massacre.'

In those final moments when facing death, most people are brought to tears. Some from pondering their eternal existence, or lack thereof; others from contemplating their missed opportunities or things they might have done. Still others cry from the excruciating pain that precedes most deaths. But not me. I weep because I know I'll be back again someday.

My heart delivers its final beats. At least for this unholy go-around.

Thumpety — Thump — Thump.

SCABS

They said the first thirty days would be the hardest, back when they were calling it a plague instead of the invasion it was. But even then it was too late. We were all infected.

The sources we had come to rely on for information vanished within those thirty days, making the world infinitely smaller. TV, the internet, news, government—even local community centers and churches were abandoned. No one remained to warn us about what came next. To tell us that they had been wrong.

Because the first thirty days were the easiest.

I woke Shay from her twenty minute slumber, all we permitted, and that only every six or so hours. The desire to stay under was far too great to allow for a longer length of time. A lack of sleep was far from the only thing causing a wedge between our relationship, though by this point we had gotten used to the changes that came with remaining alive.

Thick black goop gripped from Shay's nose onto the toughened skin of her upper lip. It was time to break her scabs open again. After helping her to her feet, I rubbed furiously at her flesh, one limb at a time. Flakes fell like leaves from a winter-stricken tree, a light trickle of blood merging with the mucous-like membrane secreted from her wounds.

She endured the exercise without a word, without complaint. Except from her eyes. Once I had finished, that crust broken open anew, I turned my back towards her, submitting to a similar treatment. I no longer flinched when her nails dug into my flesh. Pain was nothing more than background noise, the harsh squeal of a teapot whose pressure would never be released—not if I could help it. Not if we wanted to remain alive.

Remain human.

Amazing how pain and survival so quickly become synonymous.

Shay and I latched on to a group of survivors early enough that we learned what it took to keep from changing. In theory, it sounded simple. Execution, however, was another story. One by one, those of our group fell, giving in to that most human of desires. To rest. To recuperate. To heal. To seek some form of respite from what life had become.

But Shay and I were committed. To each other. To surviving. To proving our irrational stubbornness.

Or so I thought.

After weeks of barely speaking, weeks of what amounted to little more than going through the motions, Shay broke down. She asked for more time.

"Please, baby. Just an extra five minutes. I can't . . . continue like this. With this Exhaustion."

I knew what she meant. Every waking moment carried a weight like being too far beneath water. Like your body was struggling to hold itself together.

"We promised. No matter what. We won't give in."

Shay didn't respond. She had never been good at losing an argument, especially when she was wrong. In her mind, however, she hadn't lost—I just didn't know it yet.

"Ten extra minutes won't kill us. And if it does, I'd rather be dead than continue feeling this way."

"You don't mean that."

She hadn't, but the next time the alarm sounded I was plagued by an overwhelming guilt at having to wake her, almost as heavy as the enormous burden we were forced to bear. While I knew we couldn't take any chances, I also recognized the truth in her damaging words. Twenty minutes wasn't enough—that was, after all, the point of such a short period. But what would happen when neither of us had the resolve to hold out? Often I would open my eyes with Shay shaking me awake, knowing I had but blinked, that she had woken me before my apportioned time so that she could be a few moments closer to slumber herself. It wasn't true, at least I hoped not, but I understood her frustration. And anger.

Without telling her, I began to count an extra sixty seconds before waking her. Then I stretched it to two minutes. I maxed out at five, and prayed it wouldn't change things. Change her.

"Please, I'm so tired." She pleaded. Begged. Anger had dissolved, but what remained scared me more than her raised tone ever could. Desperation. "Let me sleep an hour."

"Shay, I can't. You'll turn! You'll—"

She silenced me with a kiss. The cancerous shell of spongy skin covering our lips split at the touch, pus and blood spurting, turning an act of love into the grotesquery it had become.

"Please, baby. Please. I can't think straight anymore, I just, I need an hour. Just this once. You'll see. You can watch over me, break me open if I'm going too far. Only an hour."

Despite knowing better, I gave in. I let her sleep. I massaged every part of her body in that hour, though it was anything but romantic. Breaking crust, draining fluid, slicing into tender skin. I was so intent on watching over her that I failed to notice my own body's process of healing.

When I woke her at precisely an hour's time, maybe a few minutes before, she hissed at me. "You said you would let me sleep!"

"I did."

"For an hour this time!"

"Shay, I did! You weren't easy to wake, even with me keeping you alive, keeping you . . . damaged."

She began to cry. "It felt like I barely closed my eyes."

"It was an hour. Or close to."

"Close to . . . Do you want to sleep now, or—" Her look became one of horror.

I followed her gaze, looking for the intruder I thought had certainly entered our house. "What? What is it?"

"Your back."

I reached behind and felt the ridged hump protruding from my spine. It wasn't fully formed, but it stuck at least an inch out, a beginning to the transformation.

"Did you forget? To break yourself down?"

"I guess I didn't notice." In truth, I had forgotten about the need to care for myself, more concerned with Shay's foray into a lengthier REM cycle.

"I'll break you down." She pounced on my back, scraping away the layers of hardening skin. Boils burst into fresh wounds, reawakening nerves that might otherwise have remained dormant. Every touch felt like daggers excavating my insides.

"It's not going to go away," she said.

"I know."

When she had finished, I offered both an apology and a plea, along with a proclamation of my feelings for her. It took only two words.

"Thank you."

She took hold of two of my fingers, the freshly broken skin so sensitive I almost pulled back. "I love you, too."

A week passed before she worked up the courage to ask again. By this point we were back to no longer speaking. Our waking moments full of spite, bleak intervals separated by a slumber that brought no rest and the derisive chore that kept us both alive.

"It worked fine last time," she insisted. Through the chalky substance covering her eyes I knew she had glanced toward my back, toward the ridge that would not scrape away.

"And if it doesn't?"

"Please, baby. I have to sleep. I close my eyes and you're already waking me before I've even had a chance to go under. I'd almost rather stop fighting just to really rest."

"Don't say that!"

"Then help me! Please."

Against my better judgement, I gave in.

"But this time, let me sleep for three hours."

"That's insane! I won't be able to wake you!"

We fought for hours, both of us missing our allotted twenty minute windows until we finally came to an agreement. I would let her sleep two consecutive hours, using the twenty minute alarm to switch from working on Shay to myself. In turn, she promised that when I woke her she wouldn't complain or ask for more. This was our life now, and survival required a certain amount of resignation.

The two hours were some of the slowest to pass in my life. I felt like a loved one waiting outside a surgery room for news that could only be bad. Every minute makes the most of its space when you're wrapped in the agonizing arms of the Waiting Room, a creature as real as the horrors that now roamed our world.

In her sleep, I watched her eyes move beneath her closed lids—like a wild animal, cornered and looking for an escape where none was present. I touched her eyes, forcing my thumbs into the thin crust that had covered her delicate skin. Like a creme brûlée dessert, beneath the edge of hardened flecks, a custard-like pus secreted outward with marbleized traces of red.

I rubbed her bald head—we had lost our hair the first week—painting a tapestry of lines and smoldering cracks with the excreted molten fluid. It ran down her neck, reminding me of her once auburn and wavy hair.

I followed her neck down to her shoulders, scouring deep lines in her back like the impressions made from a stick dragged through mud. And only with the lightest of touches from my quivering and bruised fingers.

Through my tightening eyelids I wept at her beauty, then raked at my own flesh like a pious priest in an act of self-flagellation.

When it was time to wake her, she wouldn't respond. I shook her for twenty minutes, slapping her and pulling her eyelids apart. I squeezed her, crushing her body with my weight, then slammed my fists against her chest. Realizing I had finally lost her, I dug my fingers so deep into her flesh I was unsure I'd be able to pull them free.

She awoke.

Screaming.

Another twenty minutes to calm her down, help her remember who she was.

By this point, I had missed my short window in which to rest by hours. My eyes were liquid fire beneath their bubbled exterior. Recognizing the state in which I was in, Shay said, "It's your turn. You need to sleep."

"Only twenty minutes. I don't need more."

Her hand caressed my cheek, breaking open the foiled skin.

"Did it help? Sleeping longer?"

"Yes," she lied. Her head fell forward, resting against mine, blood and fluid commingling in a way we no longer could. "I love you," she said.

Or so I tell myself. By this point I was already under.

The alarm brought me out, though that tide of slumber was difficult to slip free from. I sat up, immediately inspecting myself—arms, legs, torso. In the mirror: my back, head, rear. The crust was just beginning to bronze. I scraped it away like ice from a windshield.

Why had Shay let me go so long?

A sputtering sound sprung from the room, familiar and yet distant, something I should have been able to place. A burst of flames suddenly spit across the floor toward me—I scrambled from its reach, barely managing to clear the area.

The flames went out almost as quickly as they appeared. On the ground, the chaff and burnt peelings of my former skin created an outline of where I had lain. Where the fire had kept me alive. Kept me broken.

How long had I slept? And why had Shay rigged a system so elaborate?

That's when I discovered her note.

THANK YOU.

My legs gave out, my body connecting with the ground in a deadening stop.

The note was embedded across Shay's chest.

Dark smudged letters splayed across her torso in a message meant only for me. She must have scraped the skin around the letters, allowing her message to harden first—a coarse scab that opened a wound in me that will never heal. The rest of her body had solidified into a lighter tone, but far too gone for me to turn back its effects.

I didn't scream or yell out. Didn't berate her body or the shell that was left of it. I sat in that quiet room and uttered the only words that made any sense.

"I love you, too."

Her transformation continued rapidly, scabs morphing into a shell as murderously dark as night. When pieces began breaking away, crumbling to the floor like ash, I waited anxiously. I knew it would be my last time to see her.

She broke free with a shattering screech that echoed in the tiny room, announcing her arrival. Maybe her birth. We had never decided what to call it. She surveyed the room, her eyes ending on me. I had seen so many change before, but nothing could have prepared me for the look she gave—a complete lack of light shining from those bulbous eyes.

She phased toward me like a stop-motion creation, my mind able to comprehend her only in glimpses. She was suddenly before me, her black liquid eyes as big as my palms. When she sniffed, it wasn't to smell or breathe me in, it was more an absorption of my presence, tasting my reflection on reality.

I tried to see my wife within that hideous mask, her soul within those alien eyes. I'm not sure how much time passed, but I never found her.

Satisfied that my change had begun, she slipped from the room. One moment here, the next . . . gone.

It's been months since that day. Intruders come and go, breathing me in. Tasting my soul. Satisfied I'm infected, they leave, not understanding my refusal to let the process continue. To allow my body to heal. Sometimes I wonder if they aren't all the same, if it isn't Shay coming to check on my metamorphosis, questioning why I refuse to join her.

Sometimes I question that refusal myself.

But I do it for Shay. At least I tell myself that's the reason, but even now I'm beginning to forget her face. Her raspy voice and lilting laugh. Her hand holding mine, thumb drawing circles on my palm. Ones that didn't always break open flesh.

What will happen when I no longer remember her? When retracing scars brings back not memories but only a future of more pain? A future of nothing but pain. Will stubbornness be enough or am I only prolonging the inevitable?

These are questions I don't know the answer to. Questions to which I'm not sure there is an answer. I only know that it's not the pain I'm afraid of. It's what comes after.

THE LINES

Delirium.
   Recognizing Futility.
   A Dream Within a Dream.
No, way too Nolan-esque. The girl let the pen gravitate back towards her frustrated doodles. A star falling from a starless sky. The same star graced her left wrist, though inked with needle rather than pen, and served to cover the scars of her own fall into darkness. Though she hadn't been as committed then as she was now.

The first attempt had been at sixteen. A bad break up. Talk about cliché. Though, in truth, it had been much more than just finding Russ with his cock in some other girl's mouth—*Welcome Wendy, the skanking ho.*

"Welcome to Wendy's, can I take your order?"

Spoken with a drawl in a town that wasn't even Southern.

"Welcome to Wendy's, can I gargle your ball sack?"

She could turn any wiener into one hell of a happy meal; small, medium, or grande size. Eight years later and Welcome Wendy had two unwelcome kids from two disparaging fathers and had packed on an extra forty pounds, more from the french fries than baby weight. Still, word was her welcome mat remained on the front porch.

Open twenty-four seven.

The girl's first attempt had come after a series of acquaintances with death, which only made sense. The Rule of Seven states that people have to see an advertisement seven times before they'll take action or respond. In her case, it only took six:

—Mutsie, the community dog, (though really the girl had always thought of him as hers), whose remains had been strewn along the highway like an exploded can of silly string.

—The girl that lived on the far side of the park, who had always shared her smokes but never her name. An overdose.

—Aunt Silvia, (formerly Uncle Silvio), who passed from testicular cancer in a rare but poignant display of cosmic irony.

—Her Grandpa Lemons, who was living with them at the time. He had singlehandedly transformed their single-wide into a horse trailer with a permanent smell of piss and shit. A far cry from the Pine-Sol fragrance that had always graced his home and had been the source of his nickname when the girl had been a girl in more than just name.

—And a bird, a tiny sparrow, that had flown into a window of their mobile home, snapping its neck in a miscalculated instant. Something gifted with the ability of flight assigned an inanimate and immobile future.

But five deaths weren't enough to make a participant out of an observer, and so the universe played its final cruel trick, taking with it, that year, her mother.

A stroke, on her way home from work.

The stroke hadn't killed her, but the cement pillar in the underpass on the freeway hadn't been quite as forgiving.

And so, at sixteen, the girl was plunged into a master class of bills and mortgages and the blistering truth that the Beatles and their horse-shit anthems like "All You Need Is Love" were the real root of all evil. Because money sure would have solved a lot of problems.

Sixteen was too young to have your electricity shut off and your car repoed (even if it was her mother's car). Too young to find an eviction notice slapped to the front screen of your trailer where some jack-off had spray painted a dildo pointing toward a mouth and two dollar signs next to a squiggly number five. Too young to learn that in this world, you were always alone.

The first time someone had come knocking with a Lincoln in hand, the girl threw a vase at him. The second time, she had been a little wiser. Sixteen was the age she had spread her own welcome mat out. A girl had to eat somehow.

Unrequitious Love.

No, that wasn't even a word, and *Unrequited* didn't carry the same ring.

The girl fanned back through the pages in her notebook, knowing the answer was there, somewhere, just eluding her at the moment. A title for her story shouldn't be this difficult to settle upon. She stepped into the space between the lines and her longhand chicken scratch, not worrying if she would be able to make it back out. The point of writing had always been escape. It was only when she lifted her pen from the page that she realized how trapped she really was.

Between the Lines, a purple sky molted.

It wasn't stars that fell, as they had on paper; they didn't exist here. It was reality unraveling. A single cell at a time.

They blew on the breeze like ash, falling in a never-ending display. A snow globe that never needed to be turned over. The girl could always tell those who had remained here too long by the layers of fleck —what they called it—that had attached to their flesh. It *changed* them. Disfigured them. The fleck eating away any quiet beauty and replacing it with a malleable mold. It was the way those who remained here survived. Transforming themselves to look all the same.

There were no cars in the Lines, but grotesque buildings that had metastasized into mushroomed canopies, their floors stretching not vertically but horizontally. Bridges that led nowhere, and never connected. And no doors or entrances to be found. At least it kept this area clear from a heavy fleck-fall.

The girl brushed her hands against the sides of the buildings as she passed, their wrinkled stems so dry they crumbled at her touch. She had never met anyone in this part of the Lines and was convinced those that lived here never made it out of their individual buildings. Never broke free from their cocoons.

We're all trapped, she thought. Here or there, it doesn't matter.

Permanent Cocoon.

Or *Cocoon Wars.*

No, wrong genre. Maybe if she had been a sci-fi geek with a pink ponytail and thick glasses, her wardrobe consisting of shirts with comic book heroes slung across them.

The streets were desolate. Tattered and filthy pages collected at the corners of buildings and along the gutters. No street signs or lights, just one road intersecting another, a soft layer of fleck covering the ground. One trip the girl had tried to piece together some of the pages floating around. It had been after her first attempt; maybe her third. Most of those hand written pages had been filled with gibberish or insane rantings, but a few . . . a few had stood out. A few had been brilliant. It killed her to think that something so pure, so original, had been cast aside. Undiscovered. Except for the rats who might use it as scrap for their dens.

She remembered returning home after that trip, a deeper depression than normal settling in all the way to the marrow of her bones. If someone who could write like that couldn't make it, what hope did she have?

Of course, that had been back when she still believed in hope.

A Hopeless World.

A Less-Hope World.

Oh, that was terrible. If she wanted something new, something fresh, she'd have to go deeper, venture where she'd never gone before.

The street she followed would eventually lead to a village, homes made of carved out boulders where generations upon generations had spent their lives ticking out a millimeter of rock at a time. Day by day, hour by hour. The villagers there lived and died, ever expanding their houses with their tiny tools, and cared nothing for any sight beyond their own homes. All that mattered was adding another inch to their house. Another cubby to their pantry. Another child, who by the age of three would spend every minute of every day chipping away at the stone mass that had yet to be removed.

She often wondered what would happen when a family finished carving out their home, their mansions crumbling to dust upon its completion. Would they finally realize their lives, and the lives of their children's children, had all been in vain? Or would they just pick up their tools the next day and start working on a new house? A new boulder?

One visit to that village had been enough. Though she had contributed to one family's space or another's, grabbing a tool and testing her time there, she had never really belonged. A chipped rock falling loose had never given her any satisfaction, trading hours of her life for what in the end amounted to nothing more than dust. Fortunately she hadn't stayed long enough to catch the disease they called "the dream," a contagion they lived every day.

Back home, of course, once the trailer had been foreclosed on, the girl had tried her hand at a variety of jobs. Waiting on tables, waiting on managers, waiting on bosses. Waiting for paychecks that were never enough. The surroundings might have changed, but only so far as placing a colored lens on a camera alters the landscape. It was smoke and mirrors; different name tags, different insignias, carving out a millimeter at a time.

Ashes to Ashes.

No, she needed something that stood out, not just another title covered in fleck. Maybe if her name had been Ashley . . . *Ashley to Ashes* had a hint of cleverness to it, and certainly fit the theme. Still, she could do better.

Plus, she had no intention of putting her name in a title.

She wasn't that desperate.

She left the streets, moving out into the field of a toppled building. Its horizontal stories had grown too fast, too far, its base no longer able to support its girth. This particular building was only lightly covered in fleck, proving that even the newest of structures could fall. She had never explored beyond the cityscape. The straight roads and intersecting alleys were like lines on a page, boundaries that dug so deep into your subconscious you didn't even realize they were forcing you along, one step—or letter—at a time.

Beyond the husk of the fallen building, hills rose in undulating crests, covered not in grass or weeds, but fleck. Thick, unmolested patches that she would need to wade through. She wondered if she wasn't making a mistake by venturing out into the unknown. It was certainly safer treading ground she had already covered, but this might prove to be her last visit between the Lines, so there wasn't much to lose. Though, of course, every visit was meant to be the last and this was, what, her seventh trip?

Her second attempt had caused much more damage than fragmentary scarring across thin wrists, easily camouflaged by tattoos. There are moments, key moments in each life, where a half a second's decision forever alters one's path, taking one's current trajectory and replacing it with a previously unimagined road. These decisions ping you from the life you've known to some altered reality where nothing will ever be the same. Your personality, your friends, the very direction your life was headed and all you are and believe—it all jackknives, changing you in an instant into a being you would never have recognized in your former life, along your former path.

Such was this moment, for the girl.

Twenty three and fresh out of prison. A short stint—unarmed robbery and theft, though really she hadn't taken anything from the house. But using someone's shampoo and toiletries and eating their food counted as a punishable felony in the state of Arizona, especially when said person wasn't home. And you hadn't been invited. Under different circumstances they would have been paying her to house-sit while on their fourteen day Mediterranean cruise. The girl would never understand how people who had so much could be so offended by someone taking so little. She had even rinsed their dishes for them, and washed the sheets she had slept on.

But if life had been difficult before the penitentiary, the post-pen after-life was even crueler. She was branded; relegated to a halfway house where the caretakers were worse than those she had met in prison. Treated like a stray dog, to be kicked and beat down, and tossed only the occasional scrap. Employment was an impossibility, and the state only allowed so much "reintegration assistance." It wasn't long before she was applying her acquired skills at freeway off-ramps and outside Burger Kings or Del-Tacos. Waiting, sign in hand. Desperation in her eyes. Taking whatever she could get, however she could get it. Begging to survive. Another meal. Another day.

She became less than human, a splotch on a window that people just looked through. Her days merged into a single, circular mirage, until she was no longer certain where she was from or who she even was.

No one had spoken her name in over a year.

When the girl found herself on the Glendale overpass, overlooking the I-17, it hadn't been a conscious decision. It was as if she had been in a trance. All those cars with their hurried passengers, frantic to shorten the distance between here and there. But for her, the distance had been but a single step.

A step taken into air.

The medical definition of suicide states that it is the *intentional* taking of one's own life. Some definitions wrongfully add the caveat that for suicide, the person must be of sound mind. In that case, there probably hasn't been a single suicide since the earth's first waking moments. The girl still questioned her actions that day. Had they been intentional? Had she known what she was doing? Or had she simply been caught in the undertow and pulled out by the waves?

She landed on the hood of a car, its momentum quickly bucking her off. A shattered humerus and broken rib, and that was before she even hit the ground. The asphalt dug its claws into her, tearing at both flesh and face and claiming a tooth or two. Brakes wailed, and the girl waited for death to finally claim her, but her wait would be in vain. Hot air rushed past her face, blood dripped down her chin, but the car that should have lifted her body ten feet into the air never came. Instead, the back end of a trailer clipped her, its rear tire crushing her leg and wrenching her body so hard it flipped her entirely over.

Beyond the femur bone, which had been pulverized into dust and bone fragments, a spiral fracture wove all the way through her pelvis and into her lower spine.

When the paramedics finally arrived on scene, she had but a single request. "Kill me."

The marvels of modern day medicine kept her alive, but that step into air was the last she ever took. Was it any wonder she spent so much time down here? It was the only place left she drew footprints— not with her pencil, but her steps, walking the Lines.

She paused at the top of a rise to catch her breath, staring out at the landscape before her. The rolling hills dissolved beneath an immense bog, thin dying trees jutting out at odd angles like skeletal arms reaching for help.

Soon they'd learn.

To stop reaching.

Fleck fell in a heavy shroud, an oily snowstorm feeding the marshy swamp. No sign of life, though that wasn't always surprising down here. If she didn't find shelter soon, she wouldn't be able to shake off the layers of fleck that dusted her body. Without looking back from where she had come, she began the trek down the hill.

The ground became soft, each step squishing beneath her feet. She kept her footing by staying on the outskirts of the bog, ducking beneath wilted trees and stepping over diseased branches.

This Disease Called Life.

A Cure for Life.

She hadn't quite yet arrived, but she felt she was moving in the right direction. A little further, a little deeper, and she'd find what she had come here for. The title to her story. This time she wouldn't go back empty handed.

Something rustled nearby, dead brush reanimating for but a moment. She waited, one of the few things she was good at. After a long moment, it came again, fingernail branches scraping lightly against each other. And then a body crawled out, covered in fleck.

It was small, barely three feet in stature, its hair long replaced by the multi-hued sheen of dried fleck. Despite its size, it looked just like everyone else the girl had ever met in the Lines. Pouty lips, plump cheeks, an emaciated frame. A prominent forehead and large eyes leading to a chin that receded into a tiny knob, only causing the thick lips to look more pronounced. Its skin was the color of the swamp, browns and grays all mixed together like an overturned painting project.

"Hello," she said.

The thing looked up at her with wide eyes. They were always surprised to find someone who looked different, though the fresh fleck that covered the girl had no doubt already begun its transformation.

The small creature beckoned her to follow, then scampered off on all fours, its arms beating against the ground as quickly as its feet. It was so rare to find a child down here, not that they couldn't make the sojourn. They were just less inclined to discover that secret place, hidden between the Lines.

The child paused beneath a tree that had been uprooted, the only thing keeping it from the ground, the weary branches of a few scattered neighbors nearby.

The girl nodded. "I'm coming."

The child clapped its hands together without making a sound, then continued on the other side of the leaning tree. The girl followed.

The wet marsh gave way to a wasted replica, parched land and fleck-stricken trees a single gust away from collapsing. It was always dusk in the Lines, but the girl would have sworn it was growing darker. An impossibility, she knew, but one she couldn't shake.

This Darkness, Life.

Embracing the Darkness.

She felt a confidence, knowing she was getting close.

As she moved out into an opening littered with the carcasses of fallen branches, she realized she was alone, the child nowhere to be seen. She turned about, wondering if she had somehow missed its movements. Or if it had purposefully led her astray.

"Child?" She spoke with caution, someone testing a frozen lake with a tenuous step.

The rustling this time came not from brush, but beneath the woven tapestry of sticks. The child's head popped free from the ground, revealing a hidden tunnel or passageway cut beneath the littering of branches. Again, it beckoned for her to follow, then disappeared, twigs settling back in place like ripples quieting in a pond.

But a tunnel leading where?

She was deep between the Lines now, did she dare burrow further?

She brushed the fleck away from her eyelids, then wiped at her face. A cloud of scaly dust broke free, much more than she would have thought possible. Worried, she started scratching at her arms and legs, frantically breaking the layers loose, shaking her head and letting the fleck fall. Her eyes were burning from the remnants that floated around her.

Finished, she stared down at her arms. Her wrists. The smooth skin, blemished only by the discoloration of dried fleck.

Her tattoos were gone. The stars, no longer falling.

The thought burned her eyes more than the fleck ever had.

Fallen, No Longer Falling.

Was she moving closer or further away? Her reason for entering the Lines no longer seemed important. Is this why she had always turned back before? Fear of the unknown? Or fear of suddenly knowing? And more frightening was the unsolicited question, would she just become like everyone else?

The child broke free of the loose matted branches once again, its wide eyes boring into her. No beckon this time, she would have to make the choice on her own.

She drew a line in her fleck-covered wrist with a fingernail, then another. And another. Until she had carved the impression of a star.

There. I'll always be me.

She nodded toward the child, a single motion.

"I'm coming."

Its thick lips curved up in a luscious smile, then it sunk once more beneath the branches. The girl strode over to where it had disappeared, a quiet confidence returning. In her haste, she missed the locks of hair that had broken free from her scalp and lay now intermingled with the dried twigs on the ground.

It took a moment to uncover the opening beneath the heavy layer of brambles, but once located, it was clear this was no natural den. Earth gave way to stairs, carved out of rock and polished to a pearl shine. As she descended, the child nowhere in sight, the wall to her right led to a vast cavern, the stairs continuing down in a circular pattern around its perimeter. From this vantage point, she couldn't see an end to their descent.

How far down did she want to go?

Could she stop now, if she wanted?

She kept to the wall, not that she had a particular fear of heights, it just seemed foolish not to. With each plunging step she half expected the child to reappear, two or three flights down, guiding her onward, but her escort never reappeared. An occasional noise would climb its way back up; the shuffle of feet, or a loose rock tumbling down a few steps or over an edge. But this descent would have to be self-guided.

Her life as an invalid had proven more fruitful than the majority of her existence. She'd had her challenges—plenty of them—but she also discovered another side to herself that might have otherwise lain dormant. A flair for the creative. She began to write—anonymously at first, little articles sprinkled throughout the web, and later in print—but soon began to develop something of a following. Rather than having to send out a hundred queries, magazines started asking her for articles, offering repeat columns and, later, remote staff positions. She was no J.K. Rowling, but she made enough to get by which, in her world, was almost as high an accomplishment as landing a bestseller.

She was living outside of Scottsdale at the time, in a studio apartment where the elevator broke down at least once a week. Not the best of arrangements for one fettered to a wheelchair, but she made it work. She found a little new age church that wasn't far from her apartment, and got together with a few girlfriends every Thursday at Pappi's for drinks. Life wasn't all she had hoped it would be, but she was content. Happy even.

Her third attempt taught her an important lesson. You didn't need everything to go wrong in order to be brought low; sometimes it was forced upon you when everything was going right. Citing back to that whole 'sound mind' thing, she could no more control a hellacious winter storm than the drowning despair which had abruptly seized her. She wallowed for days, knowing an end had to come, she had to be picked back up. But it soon became apparent, this was how she was to remain.

She had learned from her previous miscalculations, and so this time went about a much less painful approach. Pills. Which she had in no short supply, considering her condition. She swallowed enough to guarantee she wouldn't mistakenly bob back to the surface. Her only mistake came in not realizing what day it was.

Two of her girlfriends, Jamie and Esmerelda, came by her place when she neither showed at Pappi's nor answered her phone. Paramedics were once more brought into the girl's life, denying her the one thing she had been seeking. But ultimately, it was her own fault. For having friends. A problem she had since rectified.

Befriending Death

Life's Only Guarantee

She was so close now—so close—to finally finding the answer. A title for the story she'd been working on her entire life. She was also deeper in the Lines than she had ever before ventured.

She glanced up, surprised by just how far she had come. Stairs swept upward around the chamber's walls, but she could no longer see the entrance. Below, the chamber was lit with an inordinate amount of light. She hurried down the final few rotations, anxious to find what she was looking for.

On the ground level of the chamber, the walls sparkled, glass and crystal shards reflecting back the light of a globe that floated in the air. A banquet table was set, outlandish dishes giving off an intoxicating aroma. People milled about, plates and wine glasses in hand, ignoring the floating ball as they chatted and laughed, flitting between conversation and partners like some rare exotic dance.

The girl didn't know what she had been expecting, but this certainly wasn't it. A banquet party at the bottom of a cave? And where had the child gone off to?

The fleck-covered individuals milling about were dressed in their finest clothing. Long flowing dresses, pressed tuxedos and suits, high heels and stilettos and sleeveless or puffy gowns. It almost appeared to be a costume party, except that those in attendance had been assigned different decades in which to dress, no two styles completely matching.

Aware that she was wildly underdressed, the girl began to weave in between carousing couples and flamboyant revelers, searching for the child that had led her here. Heads rolled back, cackling voices straining to top one another in ever tightening quarters as more bodies filled the chamber floor. Despite their extravagant dress, the girl was quick to note that everyone looked the same—the larger than normal eyes, puckered lips and small chins, the hairless heads that made it difficult to determine gender. Their costumes were masks, makeup meant to cover their homogenous state. But at the end of the day, when the clothes came off, they were all exactly the same.

Faces began to turn toward her, noticing as she jostled through their midst. An eye roll here, an upturned nose there. Looks and glances she had become so familiar with on the outside but that seemed exploitative down here. Someone grabbed ahold of her arm, drawing her near. The breath that spilled from the creature's mouth was horrific, a combination of death and decay.

"Is it really you?" the creature asked. It was wearing a turquoise gown gilded with sparkling sapphires.

"I don't know you," the girl said.

"Of course you know me. Sweetheart, I'm your mother." The rot and reek that rolled off her was nothing compared to the thought that this creature's words might be true.

"Everyone," the creature said, spinning about and addressing the room while tinkling a fork to her glass, "May I have your attention, please?" She waited until the room had quieted. "I would like you all to welcome our newest guest. My daughter."

The room erupted in cheers, wine glasses raising, arms and hands clapping the girl on the back, the head, the shoulders, offering congratulatory remarks.

"Really, I expected you much sooner," the woman said. "But, down here we don't dwell on regrets. We feed on memories."

She raised her wine glass high as if making a toast, but the glass, the girl noticed, was empty. So too, the woman's plate. Not a single crumb or decadent scrap. Still, the woman brought her glass to her lips and drank deeply.

The girl backed away from the woman claiming to be her mother, but the sheer amount of bodies pressed into the small space kept her from getting far. All around her, the same face wearing different garments drank from empty glasses, crunched and masticated non-existing food. The buffet table, from where such indulgent aromas swept, was cluttered with empty basins and trays, yet lined with bodies grappling to be served.

"Your grandfather's here with us," a different person said, leaning in next to the girl. She was dressed in a plunging purple gown that revealed only a bony and splotched chest.

A bald man in a tattered tuxedo moved his glass just before the girl backed into it. "Yes, but he doesn't smell like lemons here," he said, his own breath that of uncooked meat which had sat out for weeks.

Around them, every single person turned and laughed. The girl continued pressing her way through the pack of bodies, her contortionist's size enabling her to squeeze through.

A hand shot out, taking hers. "It's me, darling," a doe-eyed creature said in a red gown with an outrageously large bow on its front. "Uncle Silvio! What fun we'll have together."

A male in slacks and a dress shirt, with gold embossed suspenders, cut in. "No, it's me, Aunt Silvia. We've been waiting for someone fresh, someone who still remembers."

This time a hand raked the girl's backside, tearing her own shirt. Cold wine glasses pressed against her flesh, battling for placement.

"Mine," someone shouted.

"I need that memory!" another cry came.

The girl spun, shoving both of her hands out to widen the space through which she moved. The wine glasses of those who clambered in behind her were filled with a thick murky liquid.

Blood.

The girl's blood.

Their thick lips turned purple as they drank, a look of ecstasy strung on their faces.

"She's my daughter," a voice roared from somewhere nearby, echoed by a dozen more cries, each claiming the same thing.

The girl strode forward, pushing her way through the bodies that now lunged for her. Scratching. Tearing. Biting. Ripping away the pieces that made her unique.

She felt the memories leaking from her wounds, her fourth and fifth visits gone. Like the plot to a movie she knew she had watched but could no longer remember. Blood sloshed from the goblets around her, faces turning, chortling, imbibing, while her life dripped from their undersized chins.

This wasn't what she had come for, wasn't what she had been promised.

Where were her answers? Where was her title?

"It's all a lie," the creature who had first claimed to be her mother said, standing now before her. "All of it." She licked her lips, her goblet close to empty. "No tunnels of light or harpsichord angels strumming you to a better realm. This is it. Heaven."

Something swooshed out from beneath the woman's dress. The child, bounding on all fours.

Not a child, the girl realized. A dog.

Mutsie.

Which is why it couldn't speak.

"You wanted to see what was on the other side," the creature claiming to be her mother said. "Wanted to believe it was better than what you knew. So tell us. Is it? Better?"

Rather than answer, the girl ducked her head and plowed into the creature, breaking through the initial wall of souls staged to keep her from climbing back out. As she ran, she felt new wounds rip open, talons sinking deep within her flesh from every side. Her legs gave out and she fell, hitting the dirt and scraping her arms. She clawed herself forward, crawling as teeth sunk into her back. They were drinking straight from her now, no distillery necessary.

"Care for a smoke?" a woman asked before tearing away a chunk of flesh from the girl's scalp.

"A mother can be proud, can't she," another woman said. Or maybe it was a man.

Delirium.

Recognizing Futility.

A Dream Within a Dream.

The girl couldn't remember why she had come down here, but this time, she knew, she wouldn't be making it back. She clung to the floor, inching forward, shoulders slumped, face to ground, desperation trumped only by her indignant doggedness.

Don't stop moving. Don't stop moving. Until you can't move anymore.

The pain had graduated, infiltrating her body and assuming control over every function. Spasms. Vomit. Ending with the mother of all seizures.

She was . . . she was . . . Just . . .

The girl.

She gasped, bodies no longer surrounding her. They hung back as if an invisible barrier had formed, separating living from dead, if only for a moment. She turned over, flinging herself onto her back. The glowing globe pulsed just overhead.

Pulse.

Pulse.

Coming in weaker and weaker bursts. More time passing between each blast.

Pulse.

A memory formed. One of her last.

Sitting at her kitchen counter, razor blade held between thumb and forefinger. Ready. Finally. For this visit to be her last.

Pulse.

Her story. The title. Her *reason*. She had to finish this time. Had to craft a perfect end.

The globe lowered, drawing her into its glow, picking her body up like a sleeping child and placing her back on the cool linoleum floor of her apartment. It was slick with blood, discoloring every inch of her skin it came in contact with. Like the fleck.

The stars on her wrists had finally landed, breaking through flesh and opening a crater no suture would calm. Not this time.

Her notebook lay open beside her.

Arms shaking, the pen slipped from her grasp. She wouldn't be able to use it.

Instead, she dipped her fingers into her memories. Etched out the title to the story she had been trying to write her entire life. Her reason for leaving.

It wasn't what she had hoped for, something that would transcend time and leave a legacy for others to perhaps not follow, but learn from. But it was all she had left.

I Tried.

With a final Pulse, her eyes turned to glass, body temperature cooling, mind forever shutting down. But her memories, she kept.

THESE CONCRETE WALLS

"I drown I'm dreaming."
  "You mean you dream you're drowning."
  "That's what I said."

***

I enjoy being outdoors. Birds chittering. The rustle of leaves in the wind. The feel of the sun on your face, lighting even the back of your eyelids. These are moments that exist without requiring a frame of context, without knowing whether I'm old or young, male or female. Without requiring a setting or location with which to place such sensations, other than to know we are—for all intents and purposes—outside.

But if I were to tell you I hear a child's scream, terror and dread (and perhaps even pain) the driving force behind that desperate yet defeated plea, you would want to know where we are. A playground? A beach? A campsite? A war-torn village in some forgotten third-world country on the brink of collapse? The context allows you to anticipate where the story might be heading, allows you to prepare for the emotions that might otherwise come as a shock, the mind filling in the generous gaps in order to create a narrative that, while untrue, can at least be understood.

Unless the child's cry is just another gap. The setting not a location, but a memory of a memory, its edges faded to the point it blends in not with this background, but *every* background. Every story. Every setting.

I hear that child's scream everywhere I go.

***

"How about this time I let you ask the questions."

"Okay. Have you ever seen a shape in a cloud?"

"Sure. I imagine everyone has."

"Don't imagine. Think of one shape you've seen."

"I don't know, let's say a car."

"No. Think of a specific shape you yourself have seen. One you remember."

"Honestly, I… can't recall a specific one."

"That's how it feels. Up here. My every day."

***

They say insanity is the one trait you can never recognize in yourself. But I would argue that when you look in a mirror, whatever mask you might be wearing is always betrayed by the eyes. When it comes down to it, insane people know they're not all there. They just wear fancier masks that demand all their attention.

I don't know what I was doing in that grove of trees behind the new Ashwood development, or why I was naked, or there was blood all over my hands. And you see, already your mind is leaping forward, trying to connect pieces that maybe don't fit in the same puzzle. Instead of listening, you're making your own conclusions, writing a story I don't want any part of. A story I *wasn't* a part of.

Though I can't say as much for the man with the mask.

But one dot doesn't always lead to another. And even when they do, the shapes don't always fully take form. You may not see a car in the clouds until I suggest it. Does that mean the car wasn't always there?

***

"It's understandable to get frustrated. To be angry, even, when . . . things don't always align like they should. But you have to remember, you are the one who controls how you react to a situation. You, and only you."

"Are you married?"

"This isn't about me."

"Just—are you married?"

"Yes."

"Kids?"

"Two. Though they're grown. College and . . . well, one that wasn't meant for college."

"Would you be surprised if when you got home today you learned your family was dead?"

" . . . That's not funny."

"Your dog . . . dead. Your wife . . . dead."

"I think we've had enough for today."

"Only tomorrow you come back to work, thinking everything's fine. Helping customers, or clients, or whatever you call us."

"Patients."

"Yes, and I bet you think you have a lot of it dealing with me. But my point. What if every day you learned that those you cherish and love were gone? But every day felt like you were learning it for the first time? So tomorrow resets—you go to work, go home, only to learn—again—that they're all dead. Your family. Wait, do you have kids? Oh, you're leaving? Who's the one lacking patience now? And write this in your little notebook all you want—every time it feels like the first time!"

***

There's a bird hopping beneath the wiry mesh table near my feet, searching for crumbs. Even though I'm in a cafeteria *inside* a building. A bird. In a building. Living its life in a single room. And he's so concerned with foraging the scraps other people have dropped, he doesn't realize his whole world is a lie. That these boundaries he's living within are a made up construct. A bird that can fly, trapped in a building, because he doesn't know something exists beyond these concrete walls.

Or maybe he once knew, he just forgot.

***

"I hear there was another incident. Don't shake your head, I know you remember—*how* is another question, but beggars can't be choosers, I suppose."

84

"Someone stole my milk."

"No one stole your milk."

"I don't want to talk about it."

"Well, that's what adults do. Talk about things we don't want to talk about. We do things we don't want to do—like me being here, for instance."

"You have to be here."

"I don't—look, do you remember our conversation about how you control how you react to a situation?"

"You sound so much like your mother."

" . . . What?"

"There was—someone stole my milk."

"Do you . . . remember me? Who I am? Come on, you were just here. Look at me! Please. Tell me you know me."

"I know you."

"You do. Who am I?"

"You're that one doctor."

"I'm that one . . . doctor?"

"Don't cry. You shouldn't cry over spilled milk. Stolen milk, however . . . "

***

In my dreams, I'm drowning. It doesn't matter where. It doesn't matter why.

It's the only time I'm at peace.

The only time my screams are louder than the child's.

***

"I guess they want to move you. To a more secure facility. I've been— well, it doesn't matter. It's out of my hands, at this point . . . Not that you care. It's all one big blur to you."

"I want to go outside."

"Sometimes I wish I could see through your eyes. Life would be . . . well, simpler. Less complicated. Where they're moving you, I won't be able to visit as often. Though I doubt you'll notice, so what does it matter? Just—I hope you can remember past today, past this minute— this moment—that there are people in this world who care about you. Who love you. And . . . I'm talking to myself again, aren't I? Wherever

85

you go, wherever you're . . . trapped, I hope it's a good place. A good memory that you get to, you know, relive over and over. A time when you were happy. Because we were happy. At times. I think. But there I go again, thinking about myself, how this affects me. But this story— you're always talking about stories—it's not about me. Only I guess, in a way, it is. Because you're not the only one who's trapped. Hoping the walls built up around you will crumble to the ground, but never willing to break them down yourself. Looking at the future but seeing only more todays—never tomorrow—and wondering what happiness ever meant. You with me? One day my kids will probably be sitting where I am now, staring at the ghost of a man who's nothing but a shell. I wonder if they'll look hard enough. If they'll realize the truth. That they're only staring back at themselves. You can always tell by looking in the eyes. God, I still hear that child's scream."

"Do you dream you're drowning?"

"I drown I'm dreaming."

"That's what I said."

STILL BORN

The gift was hidden in an unremarkable bag. Neither pink nor blue—Samantha was adamant about not finding out the sex of the baby beforehand; Joel, who as a child would search every closet and crawl space for Christmas presents, feigned indifference. At their last ultrasound however, he asked their nurse Tessie, though he always thought of her as Chesty, (for obvious reasons), to print out the pictures and seal them in an envelope. For scrapbooking one day. That day came fourteen minutes later. In the bathroom just outside the doctor's office, Joel tore into the envelope. He skipped over the pictures of the alien head and went straight to the money shot. Fist pump. He knew what that little kickstand meant, though had Sam been open to finding out the sex, Chesty would have explained it was actually the labia and they were having a girl.

The bag the gift came in was a light yellow, adorned with green decorative leaves. Not fabric leaves or sparkly leaves. No bejeweled leaves.

It was sturdy, of a quality paper, neither cheap nor expensive. The only statement it made regarding who had purchased it, if indeed it had been purchased, was that the bag was unimportant. Though its contents were not quite the same.

The gift appeared rather ordinary. Something you would expect to receive at a shower.

It was untampered with, wrapped in a hard plastic casing, the kind that threatens to rip your finger clean off should you attempt to open it without scissors.

No price tag, but really Joel's mother was the only person that tacky. Joel thought his mother was just forgetful, but Sam knew better. Tammie wanted everyone to know what she had spent on that Evenflo car seat. It wasn't even the right one—they had registered for a light green one with circus animals on it. Very neutral. This one was light blue with patterned cars and trucks. Sam put on her fake smile when Tammie balked, claiming she thought she had picked out the green one, but oh well, blue was neutral too.

What Sam didn't know was that Joel had shared his incorrect discovery with not only his mother but his two brothers, their wives, a few co-workers, friends of co-workers, even the girl with the rat-like eyes he bought coffee from every morning.

The only truly remarkable thing about the gift, and had anyone really thought about it, they would have realized the oddity, was what it lacked: A name tag. Or card.

A few women had dropped gifts by prior to the party, claiming to be much busier than they actually were. But even those gifts had name tags attached. Big neon signs with arrows announcing their names.

"This present is from me."

"Look how thoughtful I was, I crocheted a blanket, who else takes that kind of time?" (Five hand-made blankets, crocheted or otherwise).

"I bought this matching outfit for baby and mommy!" (Eleven matching outfits; Joel just grateful there hadn't been a match for him).

Binkies, diapers, bottles, bottle warmers, Bumbos, Bjorns, and enough sexless clothing to dress a hermaphrodite for three childhoods.

The gift that no one claimed, the gift in the unremarkable bag, it had its moment of "oohs" and "aahs," but without someone to take credit, the moment passed quicker than most. The gift was laid on the table next to the other forgettable presents.

Though this was a gift that would not be forgotten.

I.

Sam couldn't wait for Joel to get home from work. She stood in the baby's room and took inventory. Everything was perfect.

The crib had been assembled by a neighbor's son, on leave from the service for two weeks. Joel hated putting things together and, truthfully, Sam hated letting him. Putting up with the defects in his projects was never as bad as the dark mood it would put him in. No, the twenty bucks had been a smart investment.

The mobile above the crib spun, sea horses dancing and twirling. "Twinkle, Twinkle" eked out in that haunting tone only found in baby toys and funeral homes. Bumper pads on the crib suggested an underwater theme, as if the crib were really a bubble in a live aquarium.

A changing table and small dresser were against the opposite wall, wooden rocking chair in the corner beneath the window—a gift from Sam's parents, though they hadn't made the shower. Shelves on the walls with empty picture frames hinted of all the memories so soon to come.

Two weeks.

Sam rubbed her engorged belly, hoping for a reaction. She loved that feeling of life within kicking out, already trying to prove to the world its existence, that she belonged, that she could make a difference. After all isn't that what we all believe, that we can make a difference?

Sam didn't know if it was a she, but she always referred to it as such, at least to herself. It felt wrong to call that living thing inside her an "it" this close to delivery.

After carrying her for ten months, (whoever started that rumor of nine months didn't know how to divide forty weeks), Sam felt a mother's intuition. She knew this little infant girl—if it was a girl— almost as well as she knew herself.

Baby must still be asleep.

She hadn't been feeling her as much lately, but everyone told her that was normal. As the baby grew, she had less room to move and kick.

Probably getting ready to take the plunge right now—head down, arms back, feet tucked in. Maybe she'd even hear a recorded voice like at Disneyland: *"Permaneced sentados por favor. Keep your arms and legs inside throughout the remainder of the ride."*

And what a ride it would be.

She glanced at the mermaid clock on the wall. Another two hours, at least, before Joel got home. She hit the lights and started down the hall, but found herself back in the room moments later. Something was off. Something, just not quite right.

She sat in the rocking chair considering every corner, wall space and shelf. Then she spotted it.

Unraveling the cord from the baby monitor on the changing table, she plugged it into the wall.

It still bothered her not knowing who had brought the gift. That one blank "Thank You" card seemed to cry out to her, begging to be sent. So frustrating.

A bright green light, like an eye opening, came aglow.

Sam grabbed the other half of the monitor, the piece that looked like a toy walkie-talkie. This end required batteries, though the matching light was already lit. Must have come with them. She carried the portable receptor out with her, pausing at the door.

A small kick from inside.

Finally!

She smiled, closing the door behind her. It was the last kick she ever felt.

II.

Two weeks later the neighbor's son returned to his squadron in Northern Texas and Sam delivered a lifeless baby girl. Joel held her hand the entire six-and-a-half hours of delivery.

Three days later a funeral was held. A tiny casket, one of the universe's cruelest jokes, was laid into the earth and covered. There was no handholding.

Family and loved ones stayed another few days, though for all their good intentions Sam just wished they would leave. Especially Tammie. If she even looked at Sam's belly, which still looked like she was expecting, one more time and started to cry, Sam knew she would have to murder her mother-in-law.

Eventually everyone went their way, expecting life to move on. Expecting it from experience; like a small stream. Throw a boulder in, the water doesn't stop, it just finds its way around. And for everyone else, life kept moving. The boulder left far in the distance—still there, still sad—was an event in the past and the waters were pushing them forward.

But Sam and Joel had stopped moving. They were stuck on the bottom of that boulder and quietly watched as their lives, or the lives they were supposed to live, moved forward on that stream without them.

Joel went back to work. He only lasted two days.

His manager decided to give him a little time to "sort things out."

Human Resources, that department so foreign to human emotion, stepped in and offered him a leave of absence. One month.

One month to grieve. Shouldn't take longer than that.

One month to "get over things." As if Joel were the one with issues.

One month with zero distractions or projects to keep him from thinking of what consumed his mind.

One month to be home all day, every day. The home he should be hearing the hungry cries of a tired baby. Where he and his wife should be fretting over whether she was sleeping enough, or getting enough tummy time. The home where the birth of their child should have drawn he and his wife closer together.

Instead a wall had been erected, a far-reaching cavern dug. Even their grief seemed too sacred to share. This would be the longest month of his life.

The first time it happened was the third day of Joel's leave. He heard the baby cry.

III.

Joel lay on the couch in the same clothes he had slept in for the past two days, though who was he kidding, he wasn't sleeping. The 4:15 flashing on his Blue-Ray player could have been AM or PM for all he knew. Shutters closed tight, lights off. It was just Joel and his trusty companion. The television.

Sam wouldn't leave their room except on the rare occasion she remembered to eat. She was undoubtedly waiting for him to be The Man, come wrap her in his arms, telling her everything was going to be okay.

But Joel wasn't that kind of man.

His mother raised him not to be a liar and deep down he knew everything was not going to be okay. He even suspected this would be the beginning of the end of their relationship. All he saw when he looked at Sam was that cold and stillborn child.

Stillborn.

What a terrible phrase. That despite the baby dying inside the womb, she still *had* to be born. Like it was such a burden.

"I know this thing inside my wife is dead, but I'm sorry doctor, it still has to be born."

So the couch became his domain, his haven. He had a faded but comfortable blanket an old ex-girlfriend had made, a pillow and his smart remote that controlled every system with the push of a button. Couple of beers, (couple of cases, actually), a few bags of chips. Eventually he resorted to an old pitcher that he could pee into, bathroom breaks becoming a nuisance.

He was set. And he wasn't moving until it was time to go back to work.

Reality TV soon became a headache in the back of his eyes. Cartoons were too unrealistic, with every character walking away unscathed. The History Channel biopics were too depressing. Re-runs of sitcoms made laugh-tracks sound bored. Any team he rooted for immediately started to lose. And that's when it happened—it got personal.

Joel turned the channel. Some sort of "CSI" spin-off. He preferred coming in halfway through these procedurals—it required less work. Half the time he wouldn't even know there was a twist in the plot.

The too-hot-to-be-an-investigator Blonde had just received a lead, someone coming in to confess. She walked through a door and there, handcuffed behind a table in a cold room with a mirror everyone knows people are watching behind, was Joel.

He looked terrible. Whiskered face far past the point of being "cute," eyes swollen and shadowed like he had lost a fight. Or several.

Joel wasn't surprised to find himself on TV. His thoughts had been lucid, dreams and regrets colliding so quickly he wouldn't have been surprised if the next Big Bang occurred over his head.

The Investigator crossed the room. "I heard you want to talk."

On screen, Joel looked down. "It's my fault the baby died."

"I'm listening."

"Sam kept saying something was wrong and I didn't listen. I mean, we told the doctor she hadn't been feeling much movement, but he said it was normal."

On screen he paused, wiping away grimy tears.

"She knew. She knew something was wrong and I kept her from going to the hospital. I looked into her eyes and told her, convinced her, that everything was alright. She was overreacting. There was nothing to worry about."

He laughed, a hollow, empty laugh. "I'm good at that, you know. Convincing people. Just can't convince myself."

The investigator nodded. She had what she needed.

At home, Joel felt the nausea that comes from witnessing your best friend betray you. He had nowhere left to run. Especially while remaining stationary on the couch.

He changed the channel.

A crowd cheered, carnival music playing. That comedian that had replaced Bob Barker, the one that wasn't funny, beckoned to someone in the audience. This looked to be part of his pre-diet days.

The Price is Right. Joel hadn't seen an episode since big Bob stepped down.

On screen, Joel ran down from the audience benches, hands to mouth in a ridiculous attempt at looking surprised. "I'm so excited to be here!" he said.

"Well you should be, Joel. You should be. Now I understand you and your wife recently lost a child."

"That's right."

"And is your wife here today?"

"No, I can't get her to leave her room. It . . . it's been difficult for us. I thought maybe if I got on the show I could, you know, fix things. Between us."

"That's a big expectation from a little game show," the host said, pausing, "but that's exactly what we're aiming to do! Now, let's see that showcase!"

The screams from the audience sounded like tortured souls crying from the depths of hell. Joel didn't know what was coming, but he knew it couldn't be good.

The TV host put an arm around TV Joel and led him to a rotating wall that spun slowly around. "Joel, today you are in for a treat. Because this showcase includes—"

The room spun into view.

"A beautiful baby's room!"

The announcer's deep voice cut in as Joel watched an exact replica of their daughter's room presented on syndicated television.

"That's right, everything you see here—this beautiful rosewood crib, already put together by a friendly neighbor; the hard oak rocking chair, a gift from mom and dad. Dressers, changing table, and decorations for that "under the sea" feel, but wait—there's more!"

TV Joel clapped happily along with the audience. At home, Joel swallowed the bile trying to climb out his throat.

The announcer continued. "It also comes with its very own twenty-four carat gold-plated baby!"

A camera zoomed in on the crib. A perfect replica of their baby girl's lifeless body, cast in a shiny metallic mold, lay within. It was one of the most horrific things Joel had ever seen in his life—so horrific, he couldn't take his eyes from it.

The announcer's voice became louder, deeper, no longer coming from the TV but emanating straight out of Joel's already throbbing head.

"That's right, we have the solution to fixing your marriage right here! This golden baby not only looks real. She is real! Feed her and she'll grow. Play with her and she'll respond. And when you need some time away—because we know you were scared of what a baby might do to your relationship, your spontaneity—just set her in her room! No babysitter required. She's there when you want her, and when you don't? Set her aside. That adorable golden laugh will patiently wait until you return."

The host turned his soulless eyes, like marbled colored glass, directly at Joel sitting on the couch.

"So Joel, are you ready to fix your marriage? Get your wife out of her funk so she can start seeing to your needs? Because we all know you have needs, don't you? Now, how much would you be willing to bet—"

Joel pressed the button on his remote, killing the whole system. Everything shut down at once. He sat beneath the blanket, shivering. He didn't know what he'd do for the next twenty-eight days, but television was off limits.

As he attempted to drown in the cushions, he heard a faint cough, like a baby trying to clear her throat. Then the crying began.

Wailing.

Joel stumbled from the couch, losing his balance and sending the pitcher of dark piss reeling. Shoveling unopened cards of awkward sympathy and wilted flowers to the floor, he found what he was looking for on the kitchen counter hidden beneath baby's breath from a sickly arrangement. The receiver to the baby monitor.

He hadn't even realized it was on.

His chest burned, ablaze as he listened to the baby trying to catch her breath between sobs.

"Sam? Sam?!?"

No response.

Feeling the urgency of those cries, he ran to the downstairs office Sam had converted into the baby's room and threw open the door, keeping the lights off.

"Shhhh, shhh, shhh. It's okay, it's okay! Daddy's here."

Joel set the receiver on the changing table, heavy static immediately bleeding through. He crossed over to the crib, about to reach down and pick up his little girl, but stopped.

The crib was empty.

Creases like jagged mountain tops jutted from the unwashed pink sheets, pillows and toys placed perfectly. Like a museum—look, but don't touch.

The small green-lit dot from the baby monitor on the dresser was so bright it seemed to give off heat. The static pouring from the small lined speakers, unbearable.

Joel rubbed his bruised eyes. For a second, it looked like the light had blinked. He really needed sleep. He grabbed the portable receiver and walked from the room, static immediately ceasing.

Eventually he drifted off, the monitor's receiver left on the arm of the couch. In his dreamless sleep, he never registered the quiet whisper, coming from the monitor. "Goodnight, my Angel. Goodnight."

IV.

Sam had lost a ridiculous amount of weight in the past two weeks, leaving barely a hint of her pregnancy. Once that bulge was gone, there would be nothing left to remind her of what she had carried for forty weeks. Of what she had lost.

Tears leaked from her eyes. It was amazing she had any left, but that well never ran dry.

Her stomach shouted at her. They had had many conversations lately, but she couldn't quiet those pains any longer. She had to go downstairs. A quick PB & J, two minutes, maybe three, then she'd be back in bed. Maybe she'd ask Joel if he wanted one, like when she used to make his lunches for work.

Maybe.

She almost thought of putting makeup on, changing into something a little more presentable. She wiped her running nose with her sleeve. Joel would understand.

She plunged down the stairs, worn out socks practically sliding off each step, threatening to bring her tumbling down.

Let them, she thought, though she made it to the bottom without falling.

The house had a center wall dividing family from living room. Sam chose the living room—fewer steps to the pantry.

Shelves and shelves of processed food. Family had been generous before leaving.

Jar of smooth peanut butter—she hated nuts, though Joel loved them—and bag of bread, and Sam was on the move. Maybe she'd make do without the jam. Keep her from having to go into the kitchen and talk to Joel. Not that she didn't want to see him, she just . . . sometimes she liked plain sandwiches.

Decision made, she turned back to the dining room when she heard a cry. She froze, mid-step.

Probably just the TV. Joel had it blaring twenty-four, seven. Still, she waited, listening.

It came again—the distinct sound of a baby's cry.

Sam was through the kitchen and into the family room before the peanut butter and bread hit the floor. She flipped on the lights—Joel was propped against the couch with that hideous blanket, (where had they gotten that thing?), a look of surprise on his face. And yes, guilt.

"Sam!"

"What was that cry?"

Joel took what felt an eternity to decide on an answer, finally pulling the baby monitor from beneath the blanket. "It's the monitor. It keeps . . . I keep hearing a baby cry. Probably a signal from another monitor. Another house."

Sam reached out to snatch the monitor from him but Joel pulled back, her nails instead raking across his face. She seized his momentary surprise, grappling the receiver out of his hands.

"Ow! What are you—"

"Why'd you try to hide it?"

"I wasn't!"

Joel could never lie to her. Not without her knowing.

"I didn't want you to be reminded," he said. "I know that's stupid, but . . . it's been hard for me. To hear it."

"How long?"

"I don't know. Couple hours, days? A week?"

"You should have told me."

A cooing sound filtered through from the monitor. The baby calming herself.

Her heart fluttered. A flood of tears sprung. She didn't bother wiping them. Joel hadn't kept this secret to protect her. If so, why the guilty look? No, he had kept it because he wanted it for himself! She started toward the baby's room.

Joel jumped from the couch. "No, Sam, don't go in there! Not with the monitor!"

"You can't keep me from her!"

Sam rushed the baby's room, door crashing open. As she entered, the monitor started crackling like a radio signal in a canyon. She dropped it and went straight to the crib.

Empty.

Behind her, Joel reverently picked up the fallen monitor. Sam felt him, breathing on her neck. A twinge of fear, and then he wrapped his arms around her, holding her as she stared into the vacant crib. She melted into his arms, anger dissipating.

They stood there for almost an hour, gently rocking, not a word exchanged. The static crawling into their heads was strangely calming.

Only one thought floated through Sam's mind that entire hour, one sweeping idea settling deep inside, taking root. This was not how her life was supposed to be.

V.

They named her Angel. It had seemed fitting.

Angel Samantha Perryman, with matching birth and death dates on her tiny headstone.

Sam had laid claim to Joel's previous territory, so he migrated to the kitchen, discovering a subsequent appetite that could not be quenched. Pouring chocolate syrup on a stack of four Eggo waffles smothered in jam, he watched his wife sleep on the couch. She hadn't let go of the baby monitor since the day she had wandered downstairs.

She smelled terrible.

Joel paused, forkful of dripping waffles halfway to his mouth. He had been to a hospital in Costa Rica once after a boating accident with some friends. That smell of piss and death, of sickness—real sickness— only slightly covered by the too strong scent of generic pine cleaner, was now here in his home. Sam wasn't changing her pads, the dark blotchy stains near her crotch testament enough, but that wasn't what bothered him most.

It was the smell of . . . madness.

He stuffed a handful of roasted peanuts into his mouth, beard still wet with chocolaty dew. Neither of them kept track of the days anymore. There was no such thing as a Monday or Tuesday; it was all one day, one eternally long night.

His leave of absence had come and gone. Phones were powered down. Just yesterday, (or had it been last week?), the power had been shut off. That had given them a scare; after all, the monitor in Angel's room was plugged into the wall. But the green light never stopped shining.

They knew it was her, their Angel.

After one of their more intense arguments that ended with a lamp through the TV, Joel decided to find out. Sam had been against it at first, but Joel insisted. He went up and down each street, knocking on every door in not only theirs, but the three surrounding neighborhoods. It had taken several days. There were fourteen families with a child under one. Of those fourteen, eight had baby monitors. Of those eight, three owned the same brand though not the same model. Of those three, not one had named their child Angel.

Joel finished off a glass of chocolate milk, so dark and thick it could have been a shake. And that's when he heard it. Coming from the monitor.

Voices.

He shuddered.

They had both heard them, more and more frequently, though they didn't talk about it. The voices, they always called her Angel.

They . . .

Joel crawled over to the couch, listening to the muffled conversation coming from the monitor in his wife's hand.

A woman's voice: "She smiled today."

A man's voice: "Just a reflex, she can't consciously smile yet . . ."

"I'm telling you, Angel smiled at me. When I was reading her a story. 'The Little Mermaid' . . ."

Joel closed his eyes, fighting back tears. The book that right now sat untouched, unread, on the changing table in their daughter's room.

The voices grew distant. Joel hadn't realized he was holding his breath. Then they were back.

"I'm just," the Man sighed. "Tired. This isn't exactly how I thought —" and They were gone.

Joel stood in the hall outside Angel's room. With Sam asleep, he thought he could chance it. He went in, the signal on the monitor fluttered, filling the air with an angry static. Joel grabbed the book from her nightstand—he hadn't remembered leaving it there—and darted out of the room.

When he finally fell asleep on the kitchen stool, "The Little Mermaid" was still open on his lap. It was on the page where Ariel agrees to sell her soul.

VI.

"I am talking to you!"

"I wouldn't call this a conversation—"

"I can't do it anymore, not by myself! You have got to—"

"What? Tell me! What else can I possibly do? You're the one who wanted a baby so bad—"

Sobbing. "This is *not* how it's supposed to be."

They had been at it for days. *The voices.* And it was getting worse. Angel would often go ignored for hours, screaming in the background, and all Sam wanted to do was take her away from these terrible people who couldn't see beyond themselves.

A door slammed. The man probably. He was usually the first to leave.

Sam listened as an audible apparition raised her daughter out of the crib, shushing her curdled cries. It was the woman.

"It's okay, Angel. I'll always protect you. Even from him," the woman's voice said.

Sam was beginning to like the woman, though she couldn't comprehend how she never fought back. Her husband abused her, both physically and verbally, yet the woman only whispered her threatenings to Angel.

Very unhealthy for a baby.

On the monitor the door banged back open.

"What are you doing?" The woman's voice sounded like a cat backed up against a corner.

"We're going to talk."

"Stop it, Joel! You'll hurt the baby."

Joel.

Sam turned to her husband, his blank eyes fixing on hers, though he hadn't moved from his seat in the kitchen. This was the first time either of the voices had called each other by name.

It was impossible to know exactly what was going on. The woman,

Sam apparently, cried for Joel to stop, followed by whisking noises, like something being thrown.

Joel never broke Sam's gaze. Not even as they heard The Other Sam's awful cries. Was he killing her?

His voice, close to the monitor. *Joel's voice.* "Stop fighting me! I just want to talk where I can think, without this baby . . ."

The sound of something dragging, something breaking, and above it all Angel's relentless cries. The door closed, Angel's tired voice pushing on deaf ears.

Or ears unable to help.

"It's not me," Joel said, still staring at Sam. Staring through her. "You know that's not me, right?"

Sam heard the words he was saying, but couldn't understand them. "You are such a jerk."

She flew off the couch, bringing the monitor with her, and slammed the bathroom door. Collapsing on the ground, she ripped a towel from the rack and screamed into it as loud as she could.

Angel must have felt her frustration. She answered back in kind.

VII.

"We have to get rid of it."

It was the first attempt at conversation in days, and Joel knew it was the wrong thing to say. He should have said, you need to eat, or why don't we go out tonight, or something—anything—to distract from the haunting radio program that had become their life.

Angel cried as she always did, whether asleep or awake. They were probably the only parents grateful for a colicky baby; it meant more time with her. The Other Joel and Sam occasionally tried to calm their daughter, but with little success.

Joel had ascribed them demonic names, like Beelzebub. Jo-eel and Sa-im.

His wife glared at him. "You don't get rid of a baby," she said. "You should have thought this through before deciding to put your thing in me."

"That's not—" he looked away. "It's ruining us. Can't you feel it?"

"You're afraid."

"I am not—"

"Of being discovered. Who you really are, it's been a shock to us both."

"That . . ." Joel pointed at the monitor. "Is not me! And that is NOT our daughter."

He regretted it immediately. It was their daughter. He knew it. Sam knew it. So what did that mean about Jo-eel and Sa-im?

Sam laughed, a cackle unlike anything he had heard from his wife. Her face broken out in acne reminiscent of high school; hair wispy and grease stained, like a sea caught in a violent storm—locks falling and crashing, colliding in opposing waves.

Her abrupt silence was more disturbing than her laugh. "You're not getting rid of it," she said.

And Joel knew she was right.

VIII.

In Joel's dream, Sam delivered twins. Two golden-cast babies. And they were trying to eat him.

He woke to Sam screaming his name.

"Joel! Joel!"

She was hysterical. She was also sitting on the edge of the couch, quietly listening to herself scream through the monitor. Her *Other* self.

"Something's wrong," she whispered, her only acknowledgement that Joel was awake.

"Nooo! No, God, please no. Joel!!!"

"What?!" Joel cringed at the sound of his own voice, spoken so sharply. Jo-eel's anger quickly dissipated, replaced with fear.

"Oh my God!"

"She's not breathing," Sa-im said from the little box.

"Have you—I'll call 911."

"She's not breathing, Joel!"

Sam paced, combing a hand through her matted hair. Joel found his own heart beating fast, though he remained on the stool.

A shuffling noise from the monitor. Sa-im's voice shrieking—"Don't touch her!"

"We have to do something!"

"She's . . . she's gone."

Joel watched his wife break down in front of him, tears and snot merging on her face. He was surprised to find he wasn't crying. In fact, he almost felt . . . relief. Like maybe they'd now have a chance.

Sa-im's breathless voice continued, emotion gone. "This is evidence now. That you killed her."

The silence in the room echoed the silence from the monitor. Joel could feel Sam's eyes on him.

"I'm calling 911," Jo-eel said.

"I already did. To report a murder."

"Sam, I did not kill our baby!"

"Why is she on her stomach?"

"What?"

"She's on her stomach. She's too young to roll over, which means last night you laid her on her stomach."

Joel looked up as he heard his wife speak, his *real* wife. He still thought of her that way.

"You can't lay a baby on her stomach, Joel! How could you!?"

"Sam," he said cautiously. He could hear his own swallow. "Our baby already died. This isn't real."

"Of course it's real! You never wanted a baby. Ever since she was born you've been trying to erase her, wishing for our old life without her. You killed her to get back at me. You killed her!"

"I did not kill our baby!" Joel was suddenly on his feet, shaking Sam without remembering leaving the kitchen. "This is not happening, Sam! It's not real!"

Sam beat against his chest. "Let go of me!"

"Come on!" Joel grabbed hold of his wife, pulling her toward Angel's room.

"Stop it!" she screamed. "I don't want to go in there, I don't want to see—"

"No, you are going to see and then we are going to destroy that monitor!"

He had to pick Sam up, carrying her across the threshold like on their wedding night. The green dot from the monitor on the nightstand fell on the crib as if lighting center stage of a Broadway production.

Sam stopped fighting, her chest collapsing in grief stricken shudders. Joel forced her to the edge of the crib. It felt good to finally take control. He should've done this a long time ago.

"Look! Look Sam—look!"

She did.

And so did Joel.

There, lying on the ruffled pink sheets like a mermaid resting on the ocean's bottom, was Angel.

She was bigger than Joel remembered. Her thin black hair had started turning brown and curled up at the edges. Her light skin so foreign from Joel and Sam's darker complexion. She was beautiful. An angel.

She was also not breathing. Lying on her stomach, no rise or fall to her chest or back.

Joel blinked through the tears that formed, unbidden. He let go of his wife, grief consuming him. He shouldn't have to live through this. Not twice.

He heard the attack before it came.

A sharp shriek followed by a guttural cry, then a noise that could only be described as a slashing sound. Slashing through something moist. And alive.

The rise of a bubbling brook. A loud thump, followed by the noise of someone slipping, rising, and slipping again. On liquid.

Heavy breathing.

Joel looked at his wife standing next to him. Holding the monitor. *Where was the static?*

The hard plastic back that held batteries in place, though they had never been needed, snapped off like a switchblade into Sam's waiting hand. She swung it toward his neck before he had a chance to raise his arms in defense, to plead with her. Not that he would have.

The small protruding plastic tab ripped through Joel's skin as if it were a heated blade. A foreign groan fell from his lips, a belch he couldn't hold in. The last noise he would ever make. And then he watched as his wife repeatedly stabbed the now broken and jagged plastic casing into his chest. Again.

And again.

And again.

The blood seeping from Joel's neck spouted in rhythmic bursts, following the slowing beat of his heart. He collapsed to the ground with a thump.

He heard Sam slip in his blood, stand, and hit the ground again. At least she wasn't holding the baby when she fell.

His eyes focused on the green dot on the baby monitor. That light was suddenly all he could see. And in that light he realized that every road, every decision, every word or thought or choice he could have made eventually led to this moment. This honest moment where every reality collided.

He felt the river start to pull and realized he was moving past the rock as he listened to his death in stereo. His last thought was one of contentment.

This was how his life was supposed to be.

AMADO

Tap—tap—tap.

Johan sat up, grabbing hold of the steering wheel, the dirt road and broken fence as unfamiliar as how he had gotten here. He was in the cab of his Class Eight, though he felt he was still riding the slipstream of a dream he could never quite catch, an almost out-of-body sensation. He always suffered such disconnects after killing someone. Barry called them side effects.

Tap—tap—tap.

The flashlight knocking against the driver's side window would have caused most people to leap within their seat. Johan instead squinted, looking out at a full grown bear. A black bear to boot; shame they hadn't gone extinct. He pulled the key from the ignition, the cluster of dangling keychains jostling together like chimes in the wind. A crusty rabbit's foot, Betty Boop hiking her skirt, and half a dozen cheap colored plastic rectangles with sayings like, "Truckers make better you-know-whuckers." As he opened the driver's door, he made sure he got his story right.

"Mehrnin, officer."

"Please step out from your vehicle."

"The hell are we?"

Johan hefted his two-hundred-and-eighty pounds out of the cab, leaning against the door and stretching his back out. He cracked his neck, his yawn turning into a growl as he sauntered down to the pebble strewn road.

"Have you been drinking?" The way the black cop enunciated his syllables grated on Johan's nerves. Like anyone in these back parts even knew a G was supposed to follow the I-N.

"No sir, engine went out. 'Prised she didn't roll."

"Well, you are in Amado. That's Highway 19," the officer said, pointing. "I'll need to see your permits."

"Amado?"

"Population three, oh, four. I'm surprised you haven't heard of us. Your permits?"

"Yea, bingo cards are in the glovey," Johan said, scaring off another yawn. He got his papers while the officer walked around the perimeter of his forty-foot trailer, a feat that required some time. Johan remembered the days that would have put him on edge, but the belly bin where he hid the bodies was so camouflaged not even an ASE certified mechanic could spot the mods beneath the trolley.

Keeping the driver's door open, Johan tried the keys, cranking the engine. The heavy two-stroke purred like a mountain lion, shaking the cab with its motion. He'd be on his way soon as he got rid of the bear.

Tap—tap—tap.

The officer flicked Johan's papers as if they would peel back and reveal themselves for fakes. "You're lucky you didn't roll, tires going like that. Especially down that descent."

"Tires?"

"All four rears are blown. You must have hit some debris on the road. Happens quite often out here."

Johan acknowledged this with a grumble.

"There's a service station up another mile. I'll take you."

"Preeshaydit, but a good buddy's on the way."

The officer smiled, though it looked anything but natural. "Like I said, you're in Amado. Cell reception don't work in this valley, and we're pretty particular about not allowing strangers to wander unaccompanied. You understand."

Like hell.

"You can call your friend from there. Your truck will be fine."

Tap—tap—tap.

Johan knocked against the rickety door at Rocky's Diesel Repair & Towing. Set on a quarter acre of land that must have been worth all of fifty cents, even the cactus and Joshua trees were emaciated and rotting. A dilapidated house with missing shingles and cobwebs for decor had been converted into an office by hanging a wooden placard onto its front awning. It read *OFFICE*.

"Probably closed, it being a Saturday," the officer said. "Come around the side. Family lives in a back house."

Of course they did.

Johan followed the officer through a rusted gate, passing a garage to the left with three open bays tall enough for tractors, though two were clearly used for storage. In the third a Freight Shaker sat naked, hood popped like a virgin, guts hanging out. A lanky young man in splattered overalls wheeled out from beneath the chassis and watched them.

"Leukemia," the black bear said, as if Johan was unable to notice the kid's pale face or bald head. Johan gave the kid a quick tilt of the head, a courteous hello. It wasn't returned.

Tap—tap—tap.

A shadow of a face appeared behind the blackened screen door the officer hit his flashlight against. The stubborn romping of a swamp cooler set in the window made it impossible to hear the conversation between the two. Water dripped steadily from the unit, plunging into the mud Johan had unknowingly tromped through—thick shit, that wasn't scraping off.

After a comic minute of the officer yelling into the grated screen, the door popped open, dropping half-an-inch and swinging wide with a lilting moan. A man with splotchy skin squeezed his way through the narrow gap, quickly closing the door behind him. The officer introduced him as Seth, Rocky's son.

Seth wore a beige ball cap low on his head, his red and blue lined flannel and worn khakis making him look more like a hunter than a mechanic. His eyes were swallowed in wrinkles, with a gut that hung on him like a nine month fetus pounding at the door. His mustache was thin and wispy, nothing like the thick reddish rug on Johan's face.

Seth seemed unaccustomed to visitors, shuffling his feet while listening to the officer explain Johan's situation. Yes, they could help.

Tap—tap—tap.

Johan snapped the last clevis loose from the draw bar of his tractor with a final push. He collected the straps, unhitching the trailer. Stood back on the dusty side of the road, wiping the sweat from his forehead and waving to the tow truck. All clear.

Dropping his load in public wasn't something Johan liked to do, never mind the fact he had a body reeled in on the line. The insulated trolley set in the belly bin was self-refrigerated for a good forty-eight hours. Coupla tires shouldn't be more than a few shakes. He'd be out of Amado before a den of bears fell onto his scent.

Tap—tap—tap.

Johan flicked his pen against the paperwork attached to a clipboard with what looked like a bite out of it near the bottom. Did he use his real name or give them the fake one? He hadn't been thinking clear when the cop asked for his papers; had handed over the real thing. A town this small, people talk. Best not to give them reason.

He signed the form and handed it back to Seth who stood behind the makeshift counter. A delayed smile rose to Seth's cheeks, then was gone. His head came closer to the monitor the size of a fishbowl as he began typing, finger searching the keyboard like a divining stick for the whereabouts of the next letter.

"Be outside," Johan said. "Smoke."

Tap—tap.

A cigarette popped free from the soft pack of Reds and Johan brought it to his mouth, lighter already flicking its end to a smoldering glow. The nicotine hit him like a dog welcoming its master home. Johan began walking the grounds without a thought or destination. The way he preferred living his life.

Barry would be concerned; the body, after all, would have his prints on it as much as Johan's. He was debating whether or not a call would be necessary when he heard a noise off toward the rear of the back house, a light . . .

Tap—tap—tap.

He made his way toward the sound, noticing there wasn't a backdoor or any entrance into the home but from the front. No windows in the back, just a brick wall that sagged to the left, layers of dirt scaling upward in a futile climb.

The noise sounded again, a definite knocking against what might be glass. At the foot of the wall he noticed a cubby that had been buried, the edge of a narrow window visible below ground, into a basement.

He glanced about the yard; no one there to notice him. Even the hound tied to an old loader tire ignored him. He bent down, scraping away some of the dirt to get a better look into the fogged window when a hand shot out through a broken pane, wrapping around his wrist. Johan's cigarette fell, his knees giving out and plopping him down onto the dirt.

"Help us?"

It was a whisper, a child's voice. The hand disappeared back into the depths of the basement and a face appeared in its place within an inverted V of broken glass. An eye pleading, blonde hair falling over a petite nose and dirt-streaked face.

"My sister and me," the young boy said. "They're going to kill us. Feed us to it."

Johan scooted back in the dirt on his butt, putting distance between him and the window. It wasn't his business. He got to his feet, heart still thrumming in his chest. Leaning against the brick wall, he kicked the dirt back into place, smoothing it over as if he had never been there. He slid another cigarette into his shaking hand, lit it and took a long pull, ignoring the

Tap—tap—tap

in his mind. He had never been there, hadn't seen a thing. He repeated the mantra as he circled back through the yard.

The young kid with cancer stood outside the bay, Coke in hand, his shirt hanging out one side of his filthy denim shorts. He watched Johan all the way back to the front office.

Brrrrm—brrrm—brrrm.

Seth pulled each paper from the feed as the printer chugged away, finally placing them before Johan on the counter. "Won't be able to change her 'til Monday, you got a number we can reach you?"

"Thet's two days," Johan said.

"Tomorrow's the Lord's day," Seth said, wriggling his pinky finger in his ear. "And we close early Saturdays."

"Then I'll change her myself."

"You got four spares? Like I said, shop's closed. Couldn't sell 'em to you if I wanted to."

Johan remained quiet.

"There's a motel other side of town. You want me put the number there?"

* * *

Tap—tap—tap.

The innkeeper, a short Middle-Eastern woman, probably last name Patel, opened the door a crack and peered out. She had big brown eyes matching the color of her skin and wore a faded pink nightgown with undecipherable golden symbols on it. Reminded Johan of wallpaper.

He peeled off two Franklins from the wad in his pocket in exchange for a plastic keycard. Wasn't the worst deal he had made in his life, but he was sure it was pretty damn close.

Tap—tap—tap.

The eighteen inch TV had a curtain of snow on every station that a good knock wouldn't remedy. The room was small and colorless—two beds, a nightstand, sink, mirror and bathroom. If it was clean it was from disuse, a layer of dust covering furniture and fixtures. Johan hated sleeping anywhere but his cab.

"Help us?"

Not my business, Johan thought.

He lay back on the hard bed, staring at the water stain on the popcorn ceiling. He lit a cigarette and took a long drag, had already turned over the *NO SMOKING* sign next to the TV. He was going to have to do something. With no power running to his roll-out, Rocky and sons would be alerted to a distinct fragrance that had nothing to do with engine oil. He was in one hell of a jam.

"Help us?"

The words stung.

Tap—tap—tap.

He finally heard a dial tone from the black plastic landline. Rung the digits he knew as well as his own name, maybe better. Barry picked up.

"Got a ten-thirty-three," Johan said.

"Where you at?"

"Amado."

Loud music and catcalls in the background suddenly went silent, Barry entering another room. "Where?"

"Amado. Arizona."

"Hell you doin' there?"

"You know this switch?"

Johan could hear Barry sucking air through his teeth. "Stay away from Amado, Yoyo."

"They got a couple ankle biters, den't belong to 'em."

"And?"

Johan didn't respond. Barry didn't need him to.

"Damn you, I'll be there tomorrow."

"Blow some doors off on yer way."

The music shot through the receiver again before dying abruptly. Johan let the silent phone clang back into the receiver. The stains in the ceiling seemed to be changing, morphing like billowing clouds, suggesting a storm was drawing near.

Tap—tap—tap.

The reunion the next day was sullen, and they quickly migrated to the lone bar in town. The One 'er Only, its name a depressing preview, as it was the only tavern Johan had ever been to without music, patrons or a bartend wanting business. Johan had to ask for every damn refill.

Clink—clink.

They rubbed necks back at the hotel, talking through what little Johan had devised.

"What if they weren't kidnapped?" Barry asked. "What if they're theirs?"

"They're not. He said they were gonna kill 'em. Feed 'em to . . . somethin'."

"There're stories about this place. . . You're sure they don't know you know?"

"I dunno if they know." Johan blew out a ring of smoke. "I feel like this whole cock-suckin' thing is payback, you know? For what we done. What we do."

"Like karma?"

"No, just—"

"We don't believe in that shit," Barry said.

Johan could hear the

Tap—tap—tap

of a child's knuckles against the broken window pane. And between the tapping, the inner wrenching of a young boy and girl's desperate pleas to a god who had covered his ears long ago, weary of his children whining. Johan'd had enough of Amado.

"I know it ain't our business, but they's kids. Gotta draw a line somewhere."

"Hell of a place to draw that line," Barry said.

"We go tonight, avoid a bear trap."

Barry's eyes were like smoked glass one moment, the next glinting from the echo of violence that had come before and was most certainly on its way. "I'll drive."

Amado ran parallel and on both sides of Highway 19, not a single stoplight within its borders. Even street lamps had yet to be discovered in this quiet berg, leaving only the wafting porch lights from homes set far enough back from the road that their dim glow was barely visible. With the cloud cover in the night sky it made for a very dark night.

Barry rolled his Mac up alongside Rocky's, coming to a stop before they could be seen. Johan thought of telling him to stay put but knew the words would go unheeded.

"Go in barking or under the doormat?" Barry asked.

"We are in a bulldog."

"Barking it is."

Barry flipped on the headlights and shouldered the truck onto Rocky's property, the inside of the cab jolting from the uneven terrain. He swept past the front office, driving straight into the gate, which blew out at their speed. It wasn't often they did their work out in the open. Adrenaline flared.

Instead of braking, Barry kicked the engine into the next gear, barreling straight for the corner of the brick house. Johan braced himself.

Knock—knock.

The wall imploded, bricks and mortar flying, Barry's truck lifting off the ground and settling back down onto smashed bits of concrete. The raucous noise was unhinging, aluminum roof caving as Barry backed the rig up, barely managing to detach it from the colossal mess. Johan stepped down from the cab, noticing with satisfaction that the swamp cooler was no more.

Tap—tap—tap.

The heavy screen door fell inward from Johan's blows. He stepped through, a rotten stench overtaking him that the swamp cooler must have masked from outside. Candles burned, stacked on odds and ends of appliances and junk that Johan could neither name nor guess their purpose.

Movement to his right. Without hesitation he brought up his Ruger, an antique powder revolver, and pulled the trigger. A black hole appeared in the baseball cap on Seth's head. Johan put the next round in his neck, blood spraying out like a rotating sprinkler. Barry chambered two shells into his double barrel, pumping the action in one swift and oft-rehearsed move. He rounded the doorway of the next room, letting loose his cannon. Johan gazed past the two bodies slumped against the floor and coach, barely noticing the mop of gray hair soaking up the pooling blood.

The kitchen was in the rear of the house, empty but for the purring kettle on the stove. Grime hung from every wall and appliance like it had been painted on with a second coat. They found the hatch leading to the basement beneath the table.

Flick—flick.

The lone bulb sputtered to a dim glow, narrow steps leading downward.

"Help us?"

We're coming, Johan thought, taking each miserable step down.

The putrid air above was nothing compared with the stench below. Johan had to breathe through his mouth, fighting the gag reflex and his clenching stomach. The walls were moist, stringy with whatever foul bacteria was incubating in these depths. He heard Barry retching behind him.

The tapered hall opened into a single room, thirteen candles spread in a circle on the floor. Within the circle, a body. It took Johan a few seconds to realize it was his body—*their* body—the one that had been stashed in the roll out beneath his truck.

It was barely recognizable.

The head was arched back, mouth gaping, as if even after death whatever tortures had been performed here had caused a corpse to lash out and scream. The chest and stomach were torn open and hollowed out, organs removed. Though he and Barry had drained the body, blood was slathered across the floor in adjoining pools. Johan didn't want to know whose blood.

"Dear God," Barry said.

Johan stared at the atrocity before them. Whatever he and Barry were guilty of, it wasn't this. It would never be this.

A whimpering sounded from the corner of the room, sheathed in shadow. Johan approached. A girl with dirty blonde hair, no more than seven, was shackled to the wall sitting atop a filthy mattress.

The sister.

Her shirt was ratted; on her bottom she wore nothing but panties.

Bastards, Johan thought. "Where's your brother? Your brother!"

The girl's lip trembled. "They ate him . . . the walls."

Tap—tap—tap.

Johan hammered the butt of his pistol against the shackles until they clanged to the floor. Lifted the girl into his arms, telling her to close her eyes. He wondered if she'd ever open them.

"Let's get the cuss out of here," Barry said. He was always the one with the good ideas.

A shrieking wail shattered the pungent air, followed by a loud suction sound, then a body hurled itself toward Barry from the shadows. They collided, sending the shotgun skittering across the floor and Barry tumbling to the ground with his attacker. Johan's Ruger was raised, the girl clinging to him on his left, but he couldn't tell where Barry began and the other thing ended. It roared, driving Barry back, stepping for one brief instant into the swaying light of the candles.

It was the Leukemia kid.

Naked and hairless, covered in a mucous-like secretion that dripped from his face and body, he rammed Barry against the wall. Barry screamed—Johan had never heard him scream in all his life. He hoped to never hear it again.

Instinct took over. Johan dropped the girl, ignoring her cries, and traded his Ruger for the shotgun on the ground. He was beside the two men in just a few short steps, the bald unctuous kid grinning with a crazed gleam in his colorless eyes. His hands were pressed around Barry's throat, throttling the larger man who sputtered like a broken gasket.

The pump of the shotgun was the last thing Leukemia kid heard. His head exploded, splattering outward, his diabolical grin splaying into tiny frags and pieces in a mushroomed cloud. Johan dropped the shotgun and pulled Barry into the light.

The left side of his face was chewed open as if a thousand rats had nibbled their way through layers of skin and muscle. His left arm dangled barely below the shoulder; his hand, forearm, elbow, all completely gone, gnawed into a grizzled and bloodied stump.

Johan stared in horror. When had there been time for something this extreme?

"The walls," Barry said, his words curdled in blood. "Don't touch the walls!"

Johan lifted one of the candles toward the wall. Its pink and purplish membrane pulsed, blood and sinewy tissue swarming. It was alive. Tiny black beads floated upward beneath its surface, gathering toward the light of the candle. A pale arm suddenly burst through a bubble, reaching toward him, the top of a bald head beginning to crown.

Johan dropped the candle, trading it for the girl. "Keep those eyes shut," he said, stepping over the flaccid body on the ground. He gave the walls a wide berth, walking sideways through the hall and following Barry up the stairs.

"Karma," Barry said, spittle and blood foaming from his lips. He leaned against the doorjamb of the kitchen, his remaining arm pressed against the good side of his face. Johan realized they had left the shottie in the basement. They weren't going back for it.

"We don't believe in that shit," Johan said. The girl was gripping onto his side so hard he'd have indentations for a week. "I'll drive."

Click—click—click.

Johan snapped in the buckles for Barry and the girl, locking his in place as the rig started backing up. He spun the wheel, and pulled the gear into Drive. The truck turned, its circular path on a collision course with the three bay garage. Johan hit the brakes, putting her in reverse.

A crackle of gunfire—sparks in the dark, clinks and thonks sounding off the front of the Mac's heavy grille. Glass shattered, the left headlight going dark. In the remaining light Johan saw the pale face of the bald kid behind a rifle, staring back at him. It wasn't possible. But there were two of them, standing side by side. He popped the gear back in Drive, tires spinning from the sudden reversal, digging in then jolting forward. They thundered past the garage.

The truck rumbled over the yard, more shots clanking off its frame. He passed half-a-dozen men, some holding small pistols, others long hunting rifles, their pale flesh and bald heads aglow like reflecting road signs. More glass shattered—not the windshield, but the remaining headlight, casting the yard's gate and driveway into shadow. Johan hit the flashers, the blinking red lights giving him about three feet of visibility, give or take every other second.

He turned a hard right out of Rocky's and onto the open road. Half a mile down he could cross over and hit an onramp, putting Amado far behind them. Barry muttered beneath his breath, caught in a fever dream. Johan spared him a glance—his face was broiled in sweat, shirt soaked through in patches so dark they seemed black. The girl still had her eyes closed, bless her heart.

A car materialized directly in front of them in the middle of the road —Johan swerved to the left, catching the clunker by its front but barreling through, the car spinning about behind them.

What the hell?

A dry van trailer jutted out from the left, appearing like an apparition—Johan spun the wheel to the right, pumping the brakes, tires skidding. They slammed into it sideways. Johan drove down on the gas, engine almost flooding, the scrape of metal trying to keep the truck from moving past. They slid beyond its gritting claws, Johan righting the truck and flooring it. In the remaining sidelong mirror he caught the flashes of gunshots like the dying embers of a fire.

Red lights blinking. Barry mumbling. The young girl whimpering.

And Johan, for the first time in a long time, offering a silent prayer.

Pop—pop—pop—pop.

All four tires simultaneously blew, Johan recognizing what must have been an unseen spike strip lying across the road. Perhaps the same one that landed him here in the first place. This time there was nothing Johan could do. The truck shimmied, losing its traction and plowing head on into the husk of an old school bus at full impact. An eruption of steel exploded around them in one monolithic whale's attempt to swallow another.

Tap—tap—tap.

Johan came to, the young girl beating against his arm with her fist. Barry was gone, replaced with the metal edge of a bus that had torn halfway through the cab's interior. Barry's severed legs were on the floor mat, a brown apple core wobbling between them. Johan wondered if it had been painful.

The interior lights flicked on, the ringing of the open door sounding with the sparks and still settling scraps of metal. Johan dragged the girl out with him.

He heard them coming before he saw them, the

Tap—tap—tap

of shoes against pavement, only these footfalls echoed by the dozens. Pale faces and hollow eyes. He recognized a few of them—the innkeeper, faded light dress no longer contrasting with her now equally pale face, a few splotches of dark brown makeup yet to be cleaned off; the black officer, as white as the palms of his hand, dressed in uniform, face almost glowing like a ghost; the bartender, still without a smile to spare, as well as a few others Johan had seen in passing. He was surrounded, a concourse of devils birthed from the very womb of hell—the residents of Amado, now just a few short of three, oh, four.

They came for him—claws and teeth, fangs and fists; hungry little bastards.

When they were through, his body lay draped across the back of Barry's truck, almost in the same position where they used to store the bodies, in the hidden trolley beneath. From the gaping hole in Johan's torso a trickle of blood ran. It flowed over his chest, rolling along his neck and collecting on his beard, hanging upside down. The first droplet fell to the gravel-strewn road. Then another, and another.

Tap—tap—tap.

HAPPINESS IS A COMMODITY

The modern ramblings of a "Jerry-atric"
- Jerry Atkins -

The Carrot IS the Stick
August 18th

Work to live, don't live to work. We've all heard it. The new age (*HA-HA*) mantra that life is more than the invisible shackles wrapped around our ankles and wrists; that work is the pre-requisite for a life worth living; that if we didn't know the bitter, we wouldn't enjoy the sweet.

Any others I'm missing?

But seriously, in a down economy, where labor wages have been slashed and you're lucky to even have a job, it's difficult to differentiate the carrot from the stick.

I used to be happy almost every day.

Difficult to believe, I know, especially those of you who follow this blog like the lemmings you are, but it's true. But think about this . . .

YOU used to be happy almost every day.

Sure, those were different times, and Happiness was a lot easier to come by. You all know I worked for Barker and Jones as a marketing consultant, handling some of the largest conglomerates in the nation, but what you don't know is that the commercial with the parents smiling as they brought their child home from John Hopkins' Hospital? That was my idea.

Parents . . . *smiling*.

The idea had become so foreign, it was almost thrown off the table without a second's thought. But it sure worked. Happiness consumption went up 150% within middle class suburban families—a demographic which, back then, could almost afford it. People who remembered what it was like to enjoy the time they spent with their children.

Funny what a luxury that's become today. I mean, when's the last time you've passed a park that wasn't empty? Swings swaying only to the breeze; trash and overgrown weeds replacing fields that used to be green.

Let's be honest, it's rare to see parents with children even bring them outside anymore, and not because they're trying to protect their little ones—oh no! They've simply forgotten they *have* children. Forgotten not only how to care, but that care is a necessary part of their survival.

It amazes me that people still have kids, that there can be a sustained hope for a future. *Any* future. I just read a study that of those few families who still vacation to Disneyland—(*and yes, they do exist*)— 9 out of 10 must hoard every minute of spare Happiness for over a year. A year's salary! An entire year of nothing but misery, without a single glimpse behind the curtain, all to save up your Happiness for a single day; to pretend that life is—quote, unquote—*normal*.

Is it worth it? I don't know. Like most of America, my marriage didn't survive The Perennial Depression. But I have a hard time believing you can wave goodbye to your entire savings and not regret it the second your hard-earned joy is gone. I have an even tougher time believing a family can remain a family without dipping into that Happiness they're so desperately trying to stockpile.

Can you imagine? Not only having to deal with your own withered temperament but that of your kids and spouse? Day in and day out? Without reprieve? Avoiding each other; *despising* each other; feeding into that cancerous state of mind, while knowing the entire time you're just one card punch away from relief—a twenty minute respite where color replaces the grays you're drowning in, where smells and tastes and sensations you've forgot you were privy to return, and with such vibrancy you can't keep from weeping.

(*And not the sort of weeping that occurs every other minute of your damned existence*).

We all know why we do it—and no, I'm not going to get into the

Slinky Effect or the Steeper Staircase Theory; we'll save those for another day. But I believe to the very bottom of my soul that we choose to use our Happiness not to rid ourselves of misery—as necessary as that may be—but to remember why we keep going. A reminder of what we have to live for.

But that family saving up for a-once-in-a-lifetime vacation? *(An idea marketed to them ONLY while in the throes of Happiness, I guarantee you).* How do you expect them to make it there without the occasional reminder of why they're going in the first place?

You know what I'd be interested in seeing? How about a case study of all those families who have vacation goals, who decide in a seminal state of lucidity—*(HA-HA)*—that they're going to make the ultimate sacrifice for their family, not realizing just how true that statement might be. Because how many of them never make it? How many take the plunge? Fathers, mothers, packing their kids' bags for a very different kind of vacation. One you don't come back from.

There's a study you won't see any time soon.

Speaking of data, I'm assuming you've seen the Erschweile report from last year that indicated spending your Happiness sparingly was better for the psyche than blowing your wad on one big event.

"A little Happiness a day keeps Dr. Suicide away?"

Even I have to admit that one was painful. Not mine, by the way. I had been fired from B and J by the time that coifed piece of marketing marvel came about. But unless you're in the upper 1%, let's be realistic —a little Happiness a day is as foreign as a parent's smile!

I guess I shouldn't complain. I'm normally an OEOD, Once-an-Every-Other-Dayer. Something I'm sure a lot of you would kill for.

(See, there's a reason I don't give you miserable sons-of-bitches my home address).

Did you know the average American experiences Happiness just once a week now? Twenty minutes of bliss for over ten-thousand minutes consumed in utter misery. Pretty awful trade, if you ask me. And that's taking into consideration those outliers living on the street who haven't tasted Happiness in months, or even *years*. Clinging to life like a determined bug on the outside of a windshield. But just because they're holding on doesn't mean they'll be brought in.

Doesn't mean *we'll* be brought in.

Even more frightening are some of the studies I've seen—the ones that aren't promulgated on the Ad Buys of the week—that show Happiness could be becoming less effective. In which case your slave earnings won't even lift you as high as they might have just last year.

Makes you wonder if, at some point, Happiness won't work at all. What'll happen then?

And what will we become?

Remember the antibiotics era? When you could pop a pill and almost any egregious infection would no longer be a cause for concern? When doctors were an actual profession—a respected one, at that—rather than the grave robbers they've become? When surgeries were performed at someone's request, and not at the hands of sociopathic criminals or murderers?

I know, I know, now you're really thinking I'm earning that title *"geriatric."* But consider this—the reason antibiotics stopped working is because our bodies built up a natural resistance to them. We became immune—not to the disease, but to the cure. Of course, if you really want to do your homework, look at the frequency at which those miracle pills were being prescribed. It's unpardonable, when you look back at it; most doctors handing prescriptions out as if they were placebos—just to make their patients happy.

There's some irony to that, am I right?

But what's to say the same thing isn't going to happen with Happiness? Or that it isn't *already* happening? Can anyone accurately measure the level of Happiness they achieve after a punch? Would we even be able to tell if our Happiness was dwindling in its effectiveness?

You ask me, that's when the real apocalypse begins—it won't be some zombie attack or meteor strike or nuclear war; it'll just be you and me and everyone around us, with absolutely nothing left to live for. No hope of ever experiencing Happiness again.

The worse part is that doesn't feel too far off from the truth. A whiskey shot every other day won't see you through the Sahara. Maybe the apocalypse has already begun, we just haven't realized it yet. I mean did the dinosaurs know when they had entered their extinction age?

Yeah, that noise you're hearing? It's the sound of me shuddering.

Damn, I just went back over some of what I wrote and this is some bleak shit. Please, for the love of an almighty yet unjustifiably absent divine authority, don't take anything I've said to heart. I've been saving up my Happiness the past two weeks for a date I have this Friday.

(*Yeah, even us OEODs gotta drag ourselves through the mire in the hopes of a romantic evening—should I be so lucky).*

I promise next time I'm on here it'll be in a moment of clarity. The last thing you need from me is a mere reflection of the world around you. As always, hang on, and for any new readers, comments are open only to those who are punching.

(In other words, keep your Edgar Allan Poe thoughts to yourself).

I'll leave you with this final thought: Even if the carrot *IS* the stick, at least we won't starve.

The "Good Old Days"
   August 23rd

Damn, I'm good.

Less than 12 hours since the first date and I've already gotten the *"Let's not do that again"* text; you know, the one that means *EVER*? At least in our post-PC days, we no longer have to wonder if it's you or me, or you telling me it's just you and not me, but really meaning it's me, or at least leaving me to think it's me, when maybe it really was you all along.

What a mess. These days, we all know the truth: *IT'S ALL OF US.*

You, me, and who knows? The creepy parasite living in each of our brains that feeds off the joy we should be experiencing, but no longer do.

Would to God it were that easy, huh?

Thankfully—at least for you, not for my date last night—I saved a single punch so I wouldn't be just transporting you from your living hell to mine with this post. And don't worry about me—I'll see you back home in the sludge in . . . oh, let's see . . . sixteen-and-a-half minutes?

Sigh.

So while I'm in the up and up, even if it is a slightly lower up and up than it was before, I thought I'd share some of the things I *don't* miss from the "good old days," things like trying to figure out a relationship. I mean, there are some definite advantages to the new reality of our day, and maybe this can be sort of a growing list—something we continue to add to for those days when we're contemplating the old self-destruct button.

So here goes, a list of the things I *don't* miss:

- Fast-food
- Waiting in lines
- People obsessed with "celebrities"
- Cauliflower
- Receiving telemarketing calls
- Having to define "relationships"

- Commercialism—never having what you need and always wanting what you don't; and the fact that everything was obsolete the moment after you purchased it
-

God, there's gotta be more than that . . .

Oh, I know! Doing things because you felt obligated to. Like going to visit someone you really didn't want to be around, or going to a friend's house just because you felt guilty that you bailed on them the last six times they invited you over.

Seriously, when's the last time you did something *because* you feel guilty? These days, that guilt pretty much prevents anyone from doing much of anything, let alone the "right" thing. *If* such a thing exists.

I tell you what I do miss—having a pet. Something that loved you regardless of your flaws; that was excited the moment you got home; that accepted you for who you were, not who you could become. It's insane that a little flip of the switch upstairs prevents us from not only being able to feel, but being able to care, being able to recognize that something living requires attention on our part in order to remain in that state. *Living.*

My dog—and no, I can't even remember its name—lasted longer than most, but only because we had one of those massive 50 lb bags of dry feed it ripped into, feeding itself. Drinking from . . . what? Maybe the toilet bowl? I don't remember when it died, just remember having to step over its body for several weeks, until it was our block's turn for safety inspections. It'd probably still be there, if not for that.

I used to go jogging with that dog, almost every day.

What was it's name???

This whole post sort of backfired; I was hoping to leave you with a positive vibe, realizing that things aren't as bad as they sometimes seem. And yeah, I really thought that list would be longer.

You know, it's funny, but my Grandpa Hugh used to talk about "the good old days," reminiscing instead of living in the here and now. I used to hate visiting him as a kid, seriously hate it. Because the concoction he remembered of his past always made the present inferior. Lacking in taste. Just read these next sentences with a slight Southern twang, and you'll get a sense of where I'm coming from . . .

"Back in my day, people took pride in their work. Comin' home from a day's labor with sweat on your brow and grease stains on your jeans weren't something to be ashamed of; twas somethin' to celebrate.

We didn't expect nuthin', unlike this worthless generation whose idea of sweating over your bread means holding a sign on the street corner and waiting for a hand-out. In the good old days, if you didn't wanna work, you'd starve until you did want to. Nuthin' motivates like an empty stomach."

Now, up front, my Grandpa was Filipino and definitely didn't talk like that, but those were his sentiments, if taken out of context. He had a dog, too, but one that died of old age. Maybe he didn't know how good he really had it.

The good old days . . . I wonder what future generations will have to say about them. About us. Wonder if there'll be generations in the future still around to listen. Or care.

If there was one thing Grandpa Hugh was right about, it's this— *nuthin' motivates like an empty stomach.* I try to believe that's why we go about our duties, clock in for our twelve-to-fourteen hour shifts. Not because we're weak, or too mindless *not* to show up, but because we're strong. We do what needs to be done. In order to keep our stomachs, if not full, satisfied. In order to feel . . . something. And who cares if we're only able to eat every other day—or every third or fourth, or even once a week? It still replenishes us. Fills the rotting hole with something that makes us feel full. *Alive.* At least for a few moments. And isn't that all life really is? A handful of happy memories plucked from the existential stew of existence?

I'm getting down to my last few minutes here, and after the way date night turned out I think I owe it to myself to log off and enjoy these last moments of bliss before the darkness returns to reign. Who knows? I may even pop on an old mp3, listen to a song while it still sounds like music.

There's one more thing I miss—seeing a live band play. Spontaneity, talent, and creativity mixing on the stage into an experience that was so individualized despite the fact you were standing within a crowd. I guess just like Grandpa Hugh, we didn't know how good *we* had it.

As always, hang on, and for any new readers, comments are open only to those who are punching.

(*In other words, keep your weeping and wailing and gnashing of teeth to your "good-old-day" selves*).

I'll leave you with this final thought: Hey, at least . . . you know? No cauliflower.

The modern ramblings of a "Jerry-atric"
- Jerry Atkins -

Royally Effed
   August 27th

Up front, this is not going to be one of my more pleasant posts. And don't get me started on how NONE of my posts are pleasant, you all know how often I use my Happiness just to spread some non-existent joy to you sorry saps. Not that I'll ever hear a "Thank You" for it. But that's not why I do this.

So why do I do it?

I suppose everyone has their way of coping with what reality has become. Once the normal depressants or accelerants stopped working —*I'm looking at you, Jim Bean, and Mr. Lex A. Pro*—we all did what we had to do. Found something to cling to, to call our own. Initially those somethings even gave us a small amount of joy. At least, I'd like to believe they did. But now? We just keep doing them because it's what we do. Who we are.

Like most of you, I now have a government job. Pay's shit, tasks could be more efficiently completed by robots, but at least we've got something, right? A drowning man'll hold on to a twig if it's all that floats his way.

Well, like most of you, I imagine, my manager is a certifiable douchebag—one of those undeserving, untalented pricks who the lottery gods decided to alight upon in all their erratic and supposedly indiscriminate splendor. That's right, he got promoted. And while the rest of us didn't, we're constantly reminded of what we can become. The American Dream has become a universally accepted nightmare. The real problem is that none of us know how to wake up.

(*And yeah, I know I'm risking my job just by carrying on with this blog, but come on, let an old man die in peace, will ya?*)

So today, Gerbil-Face decides to pop into my cubicle—as he does every day, with nothing better to do—but this time, he actually has a purpose other than flaunting his cheery disposition and permanently manufactured smile. He drops a sealed envelope on the stand-up tray I'm supposed to believe is a desk, then waits, apparently for me to open said letter.

Government efficiency at work, folks, I tell ya.

So I unenthusiastically open it up and unfold the notice which Puke-Head could have just as easily told me about. Then, as I read it, of course, he does.

Your six month review's up tomorrow. Make sure you're punching, he says. This is a big one.

All smiles, he actually performs an about-face turn, waving two fingers in the air as he walks out of the mobile walls that comprise my living coffin twelve-to-fourteen hours of my everyday existence. I think he was even humming a song.

The bastard.

I almost decide right then and there that I won't punch for the review. I'll show up in my zombie-like state just to prove I don't have to do what he asks, that I can make my own decision, consequence be damned. But someone my age? I don't have a lot of options. The plaques and awards of the past mean nothing to a government whose only concern is your daily output. Why do you think I am where I am? As much as I hate to admit it, I lose this gig and I'm just another lost soldier out on the street, prepping for self-detonation.

Somehow I make it through to the end of my work shift, breaking down only a couple of times. There's a punch machine on our floor, and I check my balance on my way out. I figure to be safe I'll need an hour of up-time for the review, which leaves me with one extra punch I can use for the evening. Better than nothing, I supposed.

Yes, that suppose has a past participle. Just like my life is about to have: live, exchanged for *lived*.

Fast forward a few hours, and I'm home, freaking out about tomorrow's review. I can barely eat, I've got the four-thousand page manual they gave me when I first got hired open in front of me, and I can't focus well enough to put two words together, let alone an entire sentence. It's like reading German, and after another hour I'm still stuck on the same paragraph until I finally realize I've been looking at the printing company's name and address this whole time.

I am royally effed.

Deciding I'll just have to rely on my iconic wit and charm—(*HA-HA*)—I head over to the corner market for a dose of Happiness and maybe a shit-bar wrapped in a shiny package.

Off topic, but remember when food actually tasted good? Or when we'd actually choose what we wanted to eat, depending on what we felt like? Mexican or Chinese . . . Greek or Italian or good old American? A hamburger vs. a chicken-patty vs. a hotdog, as if there was a reason to eat beyond the necessary caloric consumption to stay alive? Not all of you will know what I'm talking about, but food used to provide a certain amount of joy in and of itself.

Speaking of "the good old days," huh?

You really want to get your noggin workin', consider this—people used to be employed just to create different tastes! Chefs . . . chemists . . . short-order cooks. There was an entire industry based on people *wanting* to go out to eat. Back when social experiences were something to be enjoyed, I guess.

Anyway, now that I've COMPLETELY lost you, I make it to the store, right? Looking for a quick punch to trick my body into falling asleep before the jittery spiders of doom come crawling back through my skull. But guess what? The market's reader is jammed. Or so I thought. Two more blocks of unwelcome exercise, and the results are the same. The reader isn't taking my card.

The lady behind me, who looks like death's twin sister, tries her card anyway, even though the machine clearly isn't working. Only this time, it does. I watch the tears leak from her eyes as she extracts her arm from the punch well, two reddened marks on her forearm from where her Happiness was triggered. She looks around the grimy convenient store as if she's standing in the Taj Mahal. Even her breathing is different—controlled. Relaxed.

Oh, I almost forgot what it's like, she says.

I shove my way back in front of the line and stick my arm in, swiping my card. Some computerized meaningless jargon flashes on the display, nothing dropping from within the well.

After this point, I can't really tell you with certainty what transpired, all I know is that the punches that were thrown weren't the kind that bring any joy. I was either tossed out or magnanimously chose to leave on my own accord—(and *if I was a betting man, it wouldn't take me long to place my chips on the right choice there*). I did try a few other machines out of pure stubborn pride, but after awhile I must have looked so bedraggled, security wouldn't even let me in.

So now I've got a raging headache and a pit in my stomach—(*I never did get that shit-bar*)—and I'm no closer to ever being able to fall asleep, knowing what's coming on the glorious morrow. But that's when someone else is forcefully thrown out on the sidewalk with me.

He's screaming at security, ripping at the tie around his neck and tossing it to the ground where he stomps on it. That's when I actually hear a few of the words he's saying.

Wait, your card isn't working either? I ask.

He looks at me, but rather than answering tells me to go eff myself. Another thing that actually used to provide its own joy.

So I'm back home now, but I'm wondering if this is more than just a random card malfunction. All the recent inflation, coupled with reduced wages; what if it's more than just a bad economy? What if we've been backing ourselves up against the edge of a cliff this whole time, only now there aren't any more inches of ground to give?

What if there isn't enough Happiness to go around?

If there was a disruption with the current manufacturing output, do you honestly think our government would tell us Happiness is in short supply? That our dark days are being extended? Or would it be easier to make the ratio of Happiness to living expenses unsustainable? To enforce a reduction in Happiness consumption simply through inflation? OEODs becoming OEOWs, for instance? Once-an-Every-Other-Weeker?

But what happens when the silos empty themselves further? When only the upper echelons receive *ANY* Happiness? Maybe we're not just royally effed, we're being effed *BY* royalty.

I don't care what you have to say about new world autonomous corporations or a non-governing government; someone's in charge. Someone has to answer. How can every manager or partner in industries as diverse as Waste Management to PMM, Punch Machine Maintenance, be happy *ALL THE TIME*? Are their salaries really that much higher than ours that they can afford to punch any time they feel like it?

When's the last time you saw your boss unhappy? Wallowing in self-doubt or defeat? Caught sitting beneath the cubby of their desk with their arms folded around their knees, sobbing, in the grip of an every day panic attack? It doesn't happen. And I don't buy into the "We Promote From Within," or the "Move Up With a Smile," slogans. Remember? I created that bullshit. You ask me, there is no reason why someone should be slumming on the streets without a punch to their name while some corporate schmuck can't remember what a frown even feels like. There's plenty of misery to go around.

Alright, enough of my ramblings. And for once, I'm going to leave comments open, but ONLY because I want to know if anyone else's punch card malfunctioned today. That's right, if you were denied Happiness today, when you clearly could have afforded it, I want to know about it. Leave your comment, tell your story.

(In other words, if you WEREN'T *denied Happiness, keep your end-of-the-world conspiracy theories to yourself—as you can see, I've got enough of them already floating around upstairs).*

I'll leave you with this final thought: Celebrate. You're not the one facing a six-month review without a chance in hell of passing it.

The modern ramblings of a "Jerry-atric"
- Jerry Atkins -

The Self-Destruct Button Requires a Hand to Press It
   August 28th

I've officially cut off comments again for those who aren't punching. Of all the bad ideas I've had—which, admittedly, are many—that was really up there. And my apologies to whoever "WidOww_545" is.

Well, I'm still here. And . . . I'm still employed.

Trust me, I'm as shocked as you are. But maybe I shouldn't be. As you've no doubt heard, about a quarter of the nation's punchcards were disabled yesterday, but if you're buying the hook, line, and sinker that this is a product of "terrorism," we have other issues we need to discuss. And no, you shouldn't expect any "bonus allotment" for being one of the "unfortunate citizens tragically affected by this malfeasance."

Seriously—*malfeasance*? What, are we in a comic book now? Man, where do I apply for a marketing stint with Ole "Honest" Abe, because someone *REALLY* needs to work on upping their PR game.

And yet, how many posts have you seen by pathetic schleps claiming they're "so happy" they're miserable because they'll pick up an extra punch or two when their new cards arrive? Have any of them stopped to consider whether their new cards *WILL* arrive?

But enough about the crap you're already sifting through. Let's get to the crap you haven't yet seen. Or smelt. Or shoved your just-washed hands into, sifting through granular shit in hope of "an extra punch."

I am officially one step closer to finding out the truth, which means *YOU* are one step closer. And this time, I've got proof.

What truth is that? you ask, with your insatiable curiosity and unconquerable desire to change the world for the better? (*HA-HA*).

Bear with me.

As was to be expected, my work review goes terrible. As in, as-soon-as-I-walked-in-the-door-I-vomited-on-the-carpet-then-sat-on-the-ground-sobbing,-unable-to-answer-a-single-question, type of terrible. A redefining-of-the-word-terrible, type of terrible. Yet the whole time, my boss's boss—an older woman, whose every part looks to have been changed out or upgraded within the last couple of years—does nothing but compliment my efforts.

She's a strange one. Micro-sculpted, surgically-enhanced; yet she seems way more in tune with things than my boss ever has. She's surprisingly analytical but without the arrogance that usually accompanies those in positions of—quote, unquote—authority.

I hate to say it, but I've never seen someone so genuinely happy. She beams, *radiating* joy, like it's some kind of pheromone naturally excreted from her meticulously crafted skin. The type of person you'd *want* to emulate. For the first time in a very long time I find myself wondering what I need to do to climb the corporate ladder. To oust my boss. To gain this woman's favor. I'm almost buying into the schtick.

Then she says something I'm not expecting. She knows about the terrorist disruption with the punch cards—I mean, who doesn't, at this point?—but she says they aren't looking to punish me for something that isn't my fault. As if, had I been given the opportunity to punch, being miserable *would* have been my fault.

So many questions pop into my head, questions I want to ask, but don't dare. Not under the circumstances. Fault—guilt—blame . . . these are the trigger words so often used in our society we don't consider how grossly they're being abused. Is it the child's fault when their mother self-destructs and they find themselves out on the street without hope of ever punching again? Is it the employee's fault that the cost of survival comes with the caveat of never having a meaningful relationship again? Is it society's fault that Happiness must be purchased rather than naturally achieved, as supposedly it once was? Is there even a someone or something to take the blame—God? Nature? The collective consciousness of what remains of humanity?

After my manager goes over my numbers, which are far from impressive, his boss actually dismisses him. It's the first time I've seen the Cretin frown or experience a moment of worry. He quickly gathers up his things and whisks past me, whistling while he goes, though even the tune feels forced. Once the door closes behind him, his boss invites me to the table. Yes, I'm still groveling on the floor at this point. In my own vomit, in case you're wondering.

Are you an OED? she asks.

OEOD, I answer. When I'm lucky.

She smiles, the light in the room reflecting off her eyes in an almost hypnotic pattern. And do you consider yourself . . . lucky?

No, ma'am. I don't think fortune or luck has much to do with anything.

Then what do you consider yourself?

Worn-out, I answer truthfully.

She rises from the table and strides toward the window, raising the blinds. Though the view isn't to be admired, she seems to take great joy in looking out over a city of desolation. The bleak gray landscape is broken by thick dark clouds rising from the streets; crumbling buildings standing as if only to prove they still can.

There comes a point in every civilization where prosperity and growth are no longer interchangeable, she says. When you've climbed every hill your ancestors dreamt of scaling, yet have failed to take a step towards the mountain you were meant to ascend. In the past, it was said our consciences prevented us from rising as far as we were able. Kept us . . . grounded, you might say. Now that conscience is a thing of the past, we enslave ourselves through other means, tied to the temperaments of a bygone era.

I'm not sure if I'm supposed to add to this conversation or not, but feel the wisest choice is to keep my mouth shut.

Do you know what an achievement is? she asks.

Something you accomplish?

And once you've accomplished it, is there a need to repeat your accomplishment?

I . . . I don't know, I say. Sometimes maybe.

Example?

Children.

Children? she asks, as if unfamiliar with the word.

Just because a couple has a child doesn't mean they check that off a list. They may want a brother or sister for their young one. To interact with.

And do you think that's socially acceptable?

I don't think society should have any involvement in such a decision, I say.

Her eyebrows rise, posing a question of their own.

Just because a child won't experience Happiness until they've reached an age of higher functionality, giving back to the . . . society they mean to take from, doesn't mean—I stop myself short. My argument is eating its own tail.

You see the dilemma? she asks, her voice freshly spun silk. There is no reason for that couple to have a second child, other than selfishness. In a forgotten age, there might have been an excuse; but in today's world, once you've accomplished something you should simply . . .

Move on, I say.

She turns from the window to admire me—and yes, I know how strange that sounds, but that's exactly what she does. Like I'm a pet that amuses her, or a child that has said something particularly clever without even realizing it.

As a species, we achieved Happiness, she says. We checked it off, and we moved on. To climb the next hill or accomplish the next task. The next wonder. Only . . . something went wrong. And so, rather than summiting that mountaintop in the distance, we continue retreading the same path; one step forward, two back. Yes, I see you nodding. You know exactly what I'm speaking of. We have become the obstacle, preventing ourselves from being able to move on. Stifling growth. Strangling our prosperity. The term, one I'm not a proponent of, but that accurately describes our state of affair—*self-destruct*—is more accurate than we might realize. Would you agree with my reasoning?

I know what I should say, know what I'm supposed to say, but I can't. Whether it's the lack of punching or not, I want this well-oiled machine before me—this *creature*, who has never experienced sadness a day in her life—to see things as they really are, not as she wants to see them.

No. I wouldn't agree.

Her mouth edges upward in a smile, as if she's surprised but not overtly so. And why is that?

Because I don't think we're the ones doing the destruction. And if it's something that's being done *to* us, then it can't be described as something we ourselves do.

As in *self*-destruction? she asks.

I nod.

I sense you have a question.

Why . . . why are you being kind to me? I ask.

Kindness . . . now there's an antiquated term. You might say I appreciate honesty.

And you don't get that from the management team you fill with joy?

Her eyes darken, though she still answers. I'll admit, there are side-effects to Happiness which are not becoming. An inability to pass critical judgement. To go against the grain. To recognize failure. Especially within one's self. I find more truth in misery than I do happiness, unfortunately. Sometimes I . . . crave it—that truth. That . . . honesty. Though most people would sacrifice their individuality in exchange for a heightened sense of joy.

Did you . . . Know . . . that I wouldn't be punching for this meeting?

It's the question I've been wanting to ask. The question I'm afraid I already know the answer to.

How could I? she says. But her tone, her eyes, her subtle nod, all tell me *YES*. She knew. May have even orchestrated the act herself. Did you know that people who are happy will do anything to stay happy? she continues. Lie. Cheat. Destroy those around them. A continuity of emotions supersedes every other goal. She lets the blinds fall closed, the surreal exterior light replaced with the artificial one in the room, equally as cold. We're having a work party next Friday, she says. Upper management only. I'd like you to be there.

I'm not . . . upper management.

An invitation has been sent and should be at your home before you arrive. I've found our conversation . . . enlightening.

When deep in the dollops of despair, there's no real way to respond to such a statement. Instead, I ask a question. One I should never have asked.

Are you ever unhappy?

Her smile this time carries a sadness, as real as the exuberance which so naturally springs around her.

I'm sorry; I shouldn't have—

Never apologize for asking a question, she says. Just know that some questions don't deserve to be answered.

Without a word or gesture, I'm dismissed. I stand, awkwardly hitting into the table and wiping at my still moist face. My boss is waiting just outside the doors, though his boss does not invite him back in. While I can tell he wants to ask me what happened, what we discussed, he refrains from doing so. No one ever said the management isn't well-trained.

Now here's the kicker—back home, not only do I find an invitation to this work-related event I have *NO* desire to attend, but included in the envelope is . . .You guessed it. A replacement punch card.

Still think the "malfeasance" was caused by someone *outside* our government?

I haven't used it; the card. Not yet. And I'm still debating on whether I will. Whether I should. After the whole conversation with the woman who never even gave me her name—(*not like I would have remembered it* had *she given it to me*)—I'm hesitant to use what I've rightfully earned, let alone any "bonus" punches.

Quite the turn of events. I mean, yesterday I would have killed for twenty minutes of bliss; today, I'm too afraid to use the punches I already have. Afraid of what I might be giving up. Afraid I won't realize it's gone.

What if Happiness is more than what society wills it to be? More than the marketing campaigns and the banner displays and the illusive treasure at the end of a rainbow that never materializes in the first place? What if it's a cage, one we willingly crawl into, tripping the locks and enslaving ourselves? What if we are our own captors?

The worse part is I'm not sure how long I can hold off. Can I make it a week, two weeks, without experiencing just an increment of joy? Do I want the life this line of thinking is leading me towards? Questions and answers; answers and questions. How easy we had it when one always led to the next.

As always, hang on, and like I mentioned before, comments are back to being open ONLY to those who are punching.

(*In other words, keep your filthy self-destruct-pushing little fingers to yourself*).

I'll leave you with this final thought: No one ever chooses gray as their favorite color.

The modern ramblings of a "Jerry-atric"
- Jerry Atkins -

The Sky Has Fallen
August 31st

It's been a few days since the last post, but know it's not because I haven't been thinking about you. In fact, you're all I *have* thought about. To the point that the posts I've written in the days between I've deleted, re-written, then deleted again.

Maintaining an outlook of optimism—or at least of *NON*-self-destruction—isn't easy when you begin to question whether the Happiness you crave, the very fulcrum our society is built upon, is the reason for the expanding darkness within our existence. Talk about a downward spiral. And trust me, the posts I deleted were MUCH darker.

You can thank me later.

I realize I'm preaching to the choir here; I mean, every other update over the past few days has been about the continued attacks—the supposed *"War on our Economy."* More like a war on the working man. The latest news spouts that approximately fifty percent of punch cards are no longer operational—*INCLUDING* the recent batch sent out to replace those that were malfunctioning. A little too organized for terrorism, if you ask me.

I could say I told you so, but what good would that do? It's not like I get any joy out of this.

(*And my sympathies to those of you missing your planned punches. Hopefully your work reviews coincide with better days*).

What you probably haven't heard about, since it's been deemed unworthy of reporting, are the riots taking place. So-Town. Acrid. Meccha. The streets are in flames. Buildings erupting with multiple self-destructions, toppling towers and razing entire neighborhoods. These areas are in government lock-down—no information coming in or leaking out, except for those of us who know where to look.

Three cities. *Millions* of people. Do you honestly think your government cares that you missed your allocated Happiness punch? *IF* you subscribe to the theory that your government isn't the one *responsible* for these black outs, as they're being called. Even for someone who makes fun of the guys crying "conspiracy theory," I have to admit . . . the sky just might be falling.

You know, when my marriage ended, I didn't want to admit it was over. Neither did Dianne, apparently, as we lived together for over a year towards the end, without even speaking to each other. Not a single word. Try living in the same four-hundred square foot home with a person of the opposite sex—or any sex, for that matter—without communicating. Without complaining, gesticulating, or even acknowledging the other person. I mean, we could have at least talked about how much we hated each other, at that point! Instead we held to the idea that if we just ignored the problem—ignored each other— eventually the problem would go away. Sort itself out. Like waiting for an untied shoe to lace itself up. I don't even remember whose idea it was to finally separate; by that point we were living on such disparate wavelengths we probably thought we already were divorced.

I don't bring this up for you to feel sorry for me; empathy is as foreign as every other rational emotion our chemically unaltered predecessors had to deal with on a daily basis. But the reason I bring it up is because it's exactly what's happening now, only on a macro level.

Our government—those in control; we've been tiptoeing around them for years. Living in the same space without ever acknowledging their presence. And they've pretty much been doing the same with us —keeping us chained to the stake in the ground and calling it freedom. Our allotted Happiness. And we keep showing up—heads bowed, hands out—not caring that we're restrained or whipped or how hard the next beating is, only that our next punch is on the horizon.

<Pant-pant . . . huff-huff . . . Another 20 minutes please? Please? PRETTY PLEASE?>

But now we've gone hungry for too long. And we're starting to bite. But the hand—it's hitting back just as hard. Maybe harder. This symbiotic relationship we thought would continue? We're realizing it's a lie.

You ask me, the black outs are just the beginning. Get your punches while you can folks—*IF* you can—because I fear the whole system is falling down. And how prepared are we really to face a future that's bleaker than anything in our pasts?

You know, I don't even know where my wife ended up. I don't know where she lives, where she's working, or if she has a job. If she's even alive. The woman I spent twenty-three years of my life with—and most of them weren't bad, most were terrific! But I have no clue where she's at or how she's holding up. And I doubt she's thought once of me since our separation.

Maybe we deserve whatever's coming. Deserve to be shut down. Turned off. Just another failed project. Maybe this is the ultimate wage of our labors—not a twenty minute jolt to our brains to make everything seem better, but a dose of reality. A no-holds, unforgivably brutal look at what our lives have become. The honest truth.

What did my boss's boss say about truth and honesty? She craved it? And why? Because it can't be found in anything we've built up around ourselves.

Our homes? Our workspaces? The dumping grounds of our thoughts in the hours between work and home? They're all carefully prefabricated; made to order; boxing us in to a system someone else has created for us. Even your likes and dislikes are more an assimilation of the world that's been drawn around you, rather than your own projections onto that world. Our thoughts have become mirrors rather than cameras. Just spitting back out whatever we're being fed.

You think about it, the real problem began when we started looking beyond today, when we started contemplating tomorrow. Looking forward to something that would come irregardless of whether we anticipated it or not. We created a false expectation, replacing the present and feelings of the moment with what we *MIGHT* feel in the future. A future that never arrives.

Maybe Happiness—*REAL* Happiness, not the junked up crossing of wires and signals upstairs—is closing your eyes and expecting nothing. Then opening them, and realizing you're still there. Still present. An acceptance that there's nothing more than simply being.

Are *YOU* still there?

I'm surprised anyone still latches on to my constant gripings and moans. As you've no doubt ascertained, I haven't punched since my last post. And now, with the riots, I don't expect I will. Who knows— maybe the government will get things back under control and everything will return to the way it was . . . the economy will improve, job markets flourish, and there'll be a reason to continue existing day after day.

Maybe.

And maybe I'll go to that work party my boss's boss invited me to. And I'll have a good time; enjoy myself. Want to do more with my life.

Maybe the sky's not falling; it already fell.

As always, hang on, and for any new readers, comments are open only to those who are punching.

(*In other words, open to less than half of you,* IF *the statistics reported are correct—I have my doubts*).

I'll leave you with this final thought: Once our divorce was finalized, I cried. A taking-away-a-favorite-toy-from-a-baby type of cry. Not because of what we lost—neither Dianne nor I lost anything that hadn't disappeared from our marriage years earlier; I cried because I was supposed to. Because it was the reaction I had been trained to expect out of such a circumstance.

So my thought is this—what if we were taught the opposite of what we've come to believe? That being sad, being "down," being unhappy, is a state of being that should be *celebrated* instead of avoided? What if misery *IS* the horizon beyond Happiness? The next great achievement in the human condition?

What if we were never meant to be Happy?

The modern ramblings of a "Jerry-atric"
- Jerry Atkins -

Punch Card or Punching Bag
Sept 2nd

I know I made it sound like I wasn't going to attend that party—hell, I had no intention of attending it; are you kidding me? Strap me down and strip the nails from my fingers with a toothpick—what can be worse than a social gathering with people you not only don't like, but *despise*?

Yet I went. I felt I had to. Not for me, but for you—I had to see what these robo-managers were like outside the regimented workspace in which we encounter them. *"The upper echelon of society"*, the escalator dream we're spoon fed, of what we can become. What we should *want* to become.

I had to go—don't you see? To find out if it was a lie.

With the supply train of Happiness dwindling and the rise in malfunctioning cards, there's one thing that remains a constant—our bosses. They're always happy. *ALWAYS*. And this is what we can become if we just work harder; get promoted; turn in our work sheets and go the distance; overachieve; put in the extra effort. Because the more successful you are, the happier you are, right? Right?

RIGHT?!?

I wish I could say wrong, but I honestly don't know. Just because they're selling us on something doesn't mean it's not worth the purchase price. But having spent years marketing products that rarely live up to their advertising campaigns, I tend to be a little skeptical. Because there's always a catch.

What aren't they telling us about our corporate elite? These men and women of power, who wear their Happiness like a jewel-encrusted crown? What secrets do they not want us to know?

That's why I went. Though I wish to God, I hadn't.

The party wasn't at someone's home or building, it was—get this—on a yacht. I mean, talk about waste. How much Happiness could have been divvied out to people on the streets with nothing to call their own, in exchange for holding the party elsewhere? A high school gymnasium, for instance, or an abandoned church?

But to them, that's the point. To spend just to prove they can.

Meanwhile, if you or I want bread on our table it'll come at the cost of what should have been an extra hour of Happiness for the week. Because yeah, guess what? The punch machines may not be working but that doesn't mean the cost of shit-bars ain't rising. Honestly, I think by the time the machines are back on track there'll be nobody left with a spare punch to call their own. But I digress.

(*There may be a lot of that in this post. Psychologists used to call it a "coping mechanism." But more on that later.*)

It's difficult to fathom the sheer extravagance of this group of elitists, but as soon as I go to the dock and clamber aboard, I realize I should not have come. This is a group of people to which I will *NEVER* belong.

Even though I'm wearing my best suit, (never mind that it's my *only* suit), I'm clearly underdressed. These people are here to celebrate success; gaudiness, a necessary precursor to their celebration. Even the way they move is as if their feet never touch the ground, gliding with ease, without the burdens you or I carry that keep us trudging along the ground. Laughter, the tinkling of champagne glasses, the lascivious flirtations; all sounds so unfamiliar to me. They rise into a single amplified note that drives deep into the meaty substance of my brain, a monotonous drone that probably causes unseen hemorrhaging, for all I know.

Bottom line: I don't want to be here.

And yes, I throw up. Three times—though only one of those isn't over the railing. And no, it has nothing to do with sea sickness. I feel like I've walked into a foreign country where no one speaks my language, where every custom and sign and gesture is so completely different as to make communication an impossibility. All I can do is look around in shock and awe, gaping at the fact that people live this way.

Feeling withered, empty, is so universal we sort of take it for granted. It's just who we are—not individually, but collectively. And in this state of despondency, we tend to accept who we are and who we aren't. Who we may never become. But take one of us and dump us into a crowd that's laughing and smiling, joking, *frolicking*; a crowd of individuals who are actually *enjoying* themselves; a crowd who would better fit an old sit-com, complete with its own laugh track—one you're the only person NOT hearing; well, you no longer feel a part of the whole. A part of ANY whole. Suddenly you're the jig-saw piece that doesn't fit within the puzzle. That doesn't fit *any* puzzle. All the laughter and gaiety becomes like screams in the night—shrill and piercing, and I just know if I don't escape it, I will never make it off this boat with a sound mind.

(*If anyone can call what our minds have become sound in the first place, that is.*)

Surprisingly, even the servants are happy. Carrying food trays and drinks, or wiping up my vomit; they seem as overjoyed as the guests they so ubiquitously serve.

When the music and dancing start, I find a secluded cubby beneath a stairwell wherein I hope to hide. Ride this thing out. Chalk it up to an ill-informed decision. Certainly not my first. I drag over a rolling cart of life preservers, but before I can escape into a dark hole of my own creating, a hand clamps down on my shoulder.

My boss has found me.

His cheeks are rosier than normal, eyes glazed with a drunken cheeriness denied us normal folk. He tries engaging me in conversation, but my grunts don't hold up to his run-on sentences. I just want him to leave. Forget he saw me, so that I can hide. Disappear. Return to the nothingness where I find—if not comfort, acceptance; if not joy, a state of social equilibrium where nothing is asked of me I cannot give.

Why, you ask? Or how could such a state even exist?

Because nothing there *IS* ever asked.

My boss looks at me oddly and I realize I probably missed yet another of his inquiries. Then he says, It's almost time. Whistling, he leads me to the back of the boat.

I contemplate diving overboard every step of the way, life jacket or not. Maybe he'll just introduce me to a few people before getting distracted and leaving me to my misery. Wishful thinking, I know.

Oh, how I know.

The music cuts out as he brings me up to a small stage next to a DJ. Beneath twinkling lights I stare out at a group of impassioned people. The crowd is diverse; men and women of all ages, sizes, races. I recall a slogan that didn't come from my firm, but is clever in its own way: *Success Doesn't Discriminate.*

We're brought up to believe that anyone can find success, as if it's a lost puppy you only need to make signs for and post around your neighborhood. But we're only seeing a part of a much greater whole. Sure, success may not discriminate against race or sex or age or religion (*or at least we're taught to believe such is the case*). But it campaigns wholeheartedly, inciting a hatred so toxic it would bring about a complete genocide of this one single demographic, if it only knew how.

I'm speaking about the poor.

I heard once that being poor is the one disease to which there is no cure. A disease that's passed down from generation to generation. But whether genetic or socially engineered, our state of being is much more complex than a single virus. And I still subscribe to the theory that if it *is* a disease, someone somewhere had to physically give it to us.

Sure, maybe that's redacted thinking, but even evolution has to make choices. One species over another. One form of thinking; one amygdala; one complex being stripped of everything that made him WANT to exist, to *be*.

Oh, but don't worry. I'm sure *you* are be the exception to the rule. Isn't that the other convenient lie we're taught to hold on to? That we can rise above our situation? That the rules apply to everyone except us?

Told you there'd be a little digression.

You'll understand why I'm allowing myself to go off on these tangential trips. And trust me, if it wasn't for you? If I didn't think you needed to know what really goes on? I wouldn't be rehashing these details. Scabs don't heal when you keep pulling them off. They just fester.

Back to the yacht.

Like an auctioneer about to hawk his newest wares, my boss smiles out at the audience and says, This is Jerry Atkins. He's a miserable man. To which the crowd cheers.

Seriously.

Jerry's divorced. Lives by himself, has no hobbies of which to speak, and his savings have dwindled down to the point that if he doesn't work, he'll be on the streets. He pauses, letting the words sink in.

At least this time the crowd doesn't celebrate my misfortunes; not overtly, anyway. Though there's a sense of anticipation in the air as these chaliced men and women look on.

Jerry, my boss says, clamping his hand on my neck, Is just like each of you were. Before you were taught *how* to be happy. Before you were promoted.

I'd love to say I hold up against this crowd's scrutiny, but I'm balling by this point. I have nothing, and this presentation of my hopeless condition is far from a pep talk. In truth, if someone handed me a gun, it would have been a quick lights out. Game over. No continuations.

I search the crowd for my boss's boss, hoping she might come to my rescue, but if she's there, she remains hidden. Unseen. Letting others do her bidding for her. A part of me—a sad, despondent part—thinks maybe this display is a precursor to something better. You know, a reminder for everyone there of where they came from, preceding an announcement that—I know this sounds crazy—but that I'm to join their ranks. Become the newly promoted. I mean, why else would they invite me there?

As we've all come to know over our lifetimes, wishes carry their own barbs.

My boss turns back to me and says, Thank you, Jerry, for coming this evening. Then he sucker punches me right in the gut.

The blow is so unexpected, I double over, completely losing my breath.

To our pasts, he says, then winds back and cold cocks me. And to our futures, he adds, spitting on me.

The crowd cheers, much louder than before, then forms a line and one by one they come. Some slapping me or shoving me down, others adding their saliva to the growing pool atop my balding head. A woman with a face stretched over her skull so tightly I'm almost surprised her eyes don't pop out of her skull stomps on my hand with her high heels, puncturing skin. Someone hits me so hard, my right eye blisters over, sealing itself closed.

This is what I was brought here for: To be ridiculed. Beaten. *Bruised*. By a group of people who will never experience the pain I deal with on a daily basis.

Once everyone has their turn, laughing and smiling as they clobber me senseless, I'm forgotten. Returned to the background of their celestial lives. At this point, I crawl back to the cubby I prepared, amidst the heavy vibrations of what must pass for music and stomping feet.

I guess I should be glad I'm still alive; I mean, they could have strung me up and beaten me to death. Thrown me overboard in little pieces for the weird fishes and whales to make a feast of. But being alive doesn't induce a sense of relief or pleasure. Not for you and me. Because being alive means we have to face tomorrow, which very well may be worse than today.

I'm given a new punch card before leaving the yacht—my second "new" card in a week's time. This one is loaded with 10 additional punches, I'm told. Three hours of Happiness in exchange for becoming a piñata to the elite.

I throw the card over the rail. Two of those pompous assholes laugh when I do. At least my life provides joy to someone, huh?

One thing I did notice—there wasn't a punch machine on board that yacht. And I've never seen the swollen red lumps on the arm of my boss, the tracks of a recent hit. So what is it we're not being told? How can a group this large have an unlimited supply of Happiness? And what can we do to take it from them?

That's right, you heard me. The only thing keeping me going right now is the desire to see *their* world destroyed. Just like they've destroyed ours. If poverty is a disease, I'm going to make sure it's catching. Infect every last one of those bastards with something they can't cure.

I went to work today. I'm not sure why; sometimes I wonder if self-destruction isn't the only Exit sign still lit up. Of course, my boss stopped in, as he always does, though he didn't mention the party. Didn't act like anything had even transpired. My face is a swollen patty of uncooked meat and he acts like nothing's wrong. Because to him, nothing is.

But here's the part I'm still trying to wrap my head around—because when I got home, another invitation was waiting for me. A party. Tomorrow night.

And I'm invited.

It's not enough to be left alone in our misery, now we have to have our faces shoved into our own excrement. Why they would even invite me a second time is beyond me—seems like this is the sort of stunt you can only pull once, on the uninitiated.

I know I try to leave these posts on a positive note, telling you to "hang on," maybe add something a little sarcastic or witty to get your minds a-whirring, but today I just don't have it in me. I'm honestly not even sure there's anything left for us to hang on to.

But I'll leave you with this final thought: If you're happy and you know it, clap your hands.

(*Enjoy the silence*).

The modern ramblings of a "Jerry-atric"
- Jerry Atkins -

Trigger Happy
    Sept 3rd

News of the riots have finally broken. About time. That much noise? That much destruction? No one can keep that level of pandemonium from spreading. In the circles I follow, they're saying within the week not a single punch card will be functioning.

NOT . . . A . . . SINGLE . . . ONE.

If you've been saving for a rainy day, better make use of that umbrella while it still works. Oh, and give up your plans for Disneyland. That dream is over.

Me? I donated my punches—everything I had remaining—to a gentleman I encountered on the streets today. Watched as his eyes filled with tears. He hugged me, the reddened bumps on his forearm still fresh. It had been over eight months since his last punch, when not only his job, but industry was terminated. He was one of the last to remain in a sinking boat, and the postal service rewarded his loyalty as corporations and governments often do—by taking everything from him, then casting his remaining carcass aside.

Eight months on the street. Who knows, another few days without a glimpse of something more than what his life had become, and he could have self-destructed. I certainly don't expect to last that long.

I joined him for dinner, eating outside the corner market. While I ate because I had to, he seemed to relish every bite, licking the shit-bar wrapper, and even asking if he could finish mine. He told me about his daughter, who he hadn't thought of in over a year. I don't remember her name, but he spoke of her with fondness. Said he worried about her. Funny how Happiness can trigger those kinds of emotions—worry, concern, regret. Words you wouldn't necessarily associate with a happy nature. But when darkness spreads its poisoned quilt over our minds, Happiness isn't the only emotion we lose access to.

He must have thanked me a hundred times, then asked what he could do to help. How he could repay me. Almost belligerently inquiring.

Understand, I didn't give away my punches expecting anything in return. I had no ulterior motives. I gave them away because I didn't want them, and I figured someone should benefit, find a little joy where I find none.

But when he asked, I answered. I told him there was a party tonight. And I had a previous obligation. And would he want to go in my stead.

I don't know why I asked him that; I'm not even sure it was something I wanted to ask him . . . it just sort of came out.

I'm not trying to make excuses, and I realize that after this post you'll probably never look at me the same way again, but it's not going to stop me from being honest. At least here, on an anonymous blogroll, I can be free from the lies I tell myself.

Am I ashamed at what I've done? Of the wheels I've set in motion? Maybe—I don't know; maybe I was jealous of how happy he felt, even though I was the one who gave away that Happiness. Maybe I wanted to see him miserable again. But worse than just the crash that follows a good punch. Maybe I wanted to see him utterly and entirely without hope. And maybe I wanted him to know that I was the one who made him feel that way. That the Happiness I so freely gave could be just as easily be taken away.

These aren't easy things for me to pen right now; slitting my wrists and bleeding onto the keyboard, all for the sake of what—your entertainment? Keeping you in the know?

And how do you know I don't have my own reasons for doing this? My own secret agenda? That the things I'm writing aren't primed to make you feel a certain way? Do a certain thing? Are any of our experiences unique or are we just regurgitating what's come before? Happiness? Emptiness? Empathy, or a complete lack thereof? We're not bringing anything new to the table. We're all copies of copies, without an ounce of authenticity remaining.

In fact, your reaction to my rants are as preprogrammed as the alarm that sounds every morning, waking you up at quarter-to-five. Thinking you could do better, contribute more? Disgusted with my self-hate while you loathe who you've become.

It's okay, I'm not angry. I understand why you're feeling this way. But what I don't know is whether what you're feeling is what you're supposed to feel or if it's rather the triggered effects of a pre-wired situation. What if, when it comes down to it, all that's running in our heads are a bunch of predetermined equations. When X occurs, Y should be felt. Why? Because it's in the equation. Though secretly I believe all our equations add up to zero.

Now that we're past the point of you asking—*How could I?*—and me trying to invent an excuse that will never hold up, we can move forward. Sure, we might no longer be holding hands, nor will I begrudge you keeping a watchful eye on me. I'll present just the facts. Make of them what you will. I give this man who lauds me as some kind of hero the address to the dock and tell him not to be late. Though he'll undoubtedly crash long before the party starts, he promises he will be there. On the life of his daughter, he says. He'll do anything for what I've given him. Anything.

Still think I'm the bad guy?

I follow him to the dock, to make sure he gets on board. Hide behind an overflowing dumpster, my heart prattling away as he walks the long narrow strip of planks toward the yacht. While he still wears the same filthy outfit, he's cleaned up where he can—shaving his face, even cutting his hair. As if any of that will matter.

Several minutes pass with him speaking to someone at the far end of the dock, and I'm sure they won't let him on. I mean, it's not like the invitation said a substitute could go in my stead. But then they let him pass, take him on board, and I can't begin to explain the feelings that swell within me. It's . . . almost like I'm punching.

I keep smiling, then letting my smile fall, only for it to rise naturally again on its own. My breathing changes, heart rate jumping, and I keep picturing glimpses of what might be, an almost infinite array of scenarios playing before me. It's as close to Happiness as anything I've felt.

I watch the yacht sail off, the reflection of the moon off it's hull eventually disappearing in the sea of darkness. But rather than go home, I stay. I can't help myself. I have to see what happens when they return.

When *he* returns.

I didn't bring a jacket or anything warm to wear, and the temperature quickly takes a nosedive, plunging me into the terrain just beyond discomfort. I pull my arms into my shirt, raising the collar to cover my nose while blowing warm air into the hollow it creates. Damned uncomfortable, but this is something I'm committed to. Seeing is believing, and believing . . . well, who would have believed I could feel like this without a single punch?

It's past midnight when the yacht returns. I reposition myself behind the dumpster and wait, trying to wipe the grin from my face. A host of men and women all done up in their fancy gowns stream past, their laughter sending chills down my spine. More of them trickle by, in smaller groups now, but I have yet to see the man I sentenced to ridicule and pain, the man I forced to take my place.

The servants come next, though they've clearly fallen. Their faces are drawn out, no laughter or even conversation taking place among them. They carry with them an overwhelming sense of exhaustion. Those in charge must make them punch before getting on the ship each night. Forcing Happiness on them in order to not bring down those they serve.

Then I hear a commotion back at the boat—a man thrown onto the dock. From where I stand I'm unable to determine with certainty if this is my man, except for the fact that he doesn't try to get up. He just lays there, covering his head with his arms as if he expects the beating to continue.

Definitely my man.

I watch with anticipation, reveling in the fact that I hadn't just lain there. I had gotten to my feet, dismissing their gift, and returned to my life. I am stronger than my new friend.

Words carry, though unintelligible, but someone's clearly talking to him. I watch a suited man set something on the ground beside my friend. Probably a new punch card. I'm right. But also wrong.

Very wrong.

Now what happens next I could never have predicted. If I had known—truly known—what was going to occur, I never would have asked that man to take my place. He crawls toward the box, then wrestles with its contents. In the next moment a gunshot rings out. Like a murder of crows, cawing incessantly, that shot circles overhead, continuing on and on and on.

No one comes to investigate. I guess I shouldn't be surprised, but I am. They know what that sound means. They're the ones who planted those feelings in his head—when X occurs, Y should be felt, followed shortly thereafter by the action. Z.

I told you it always adds up to zero.

Another half hour passes and I finally decide to go down myself. I owe it to him. And maybe to myself. After all, I'm as tangled up in this equation as he is. Or was.

I may have overstated the joy I felt up to that point, in wondering what might befall this surrogate of mine, but any remnants of Happiness have fled with the sound of that gunshot. A part of me hopes he's still alive, that the shot wasn't fatal. But that part quickly gives out as I close in on his body. He lays face down, half of his head blown off, blood seeping out in twin trails that spill over the edge of wooden planks to either side of the dock. Dripping into an ocean that doesn't care what's being added to it. That doesn't even notice. The gun that ended the man's life rests just a few inches from his outstretched hand.

He brought this on himself, I try to reason. *If I hadn't have shared with him my Happiness, the results would have been the same. He was headed for self-destruction, irregardless of my place in his life.* But all the reasoning in the world can't change the horror I feel. I may as well have pulled the trigger myself.

I force down the curled up edges of my lips. This is sad. A life extinguished.

No one stirs on the yacht; no one I can see, anyway. Still, I feel it wisest to move on. I lift the lid of the box, however, to see if anything remains within and, yep—there's a brand new punchcard at the bottom of the hinged wooden box. This one I don't throw back in the water.

I wonder now, more than ever, about the emotions I felt—or the emotions I *think* I felt. Happiness . . . Sadness . . . Were they just triggered responses? A lever so small it requires just the slightest pressure? And yet how could we fully comprehend the incredible power released by that fraction of an inch? A bullet that stops every higher function. An emotion that pretty much does the same.

I know what you're thinking, and I can't blame you. If it was possible for me to hate myself more than I already do, then I'd have arrived at that state. I can't sleep. My shift starts in four hours, and all I can think about is the sound of that gun firing. It echoes still in my head.

I wonder what they did to him on board. What ultimately triggered his self-destruction. This was a man who had survived eight months on his own—*eight months*! A man married to emptiness. Yet somehow they brought him lower. So low that he couldn't find his way back out.

This is as low as I've felt in a long time, the darkness eating at my mewling soul. Just when you think there's nowhere lower to go. And yet a part of me—a part I don't want to even admit *exists*—is fixated on the fact that I felt happy there on the dock. Really happy. No punch required. Something that shouldn't be possible in our day and age. I don't yet understand it. I'm not sure I ever will.

As always, hang on. Seriously. Our world, which we've grown so accustomed to, might be changing. And that's never for the better. I am however going to keep comments closed for the foreseeable future. With the widening swath of inoperable cards and the general mood I find myself in, I feel I'm doing us all a favor.

(*In other words, fillet me with your thoughts and mental curses all you want—for once, I don't have to listen to them*).

I'll leave you with this final thought: It only required him to move his finger half an inch.

The modern ramblings of a "Jerry-atric"
- Jerry Atkins -

You're Invited
  Sept 4th

I'm holding in my hands another invitation. It was here, in my loft, when I got back from work today. Just like the previous times, there was no sign of forced entry or proof that anyone had broken in. Other than the incriminating card itself.

The invitation's folded in half so that you have to open it, the paper itself having a weight to it. The entire thing is black, with gold lacquered swirls along the edges and gold embossed lettering on the front. It reads: *YOU'RE INVITED.*

Few words have ever been so damning.

I haven't opened it yet; in truth, I'm not sure I can handle another gentle shove towards the edge of this open abyss. Darkness, waiting to receive me. We're all invited, when you think about it. To a party that never ends. A party that never should have started.

I almost punched on my way home from work—don't ask why I went; some things we just do out of habit. Breathe air, eat food, open our eyes each morning. Mistakenly I thought work might take my mind off the death of that man, allow me to focus on something else, even if the distraction was temporary. Unfortunately—or fortunately, depending on how you look at it—the distraction never came. Every moment, every thought, is weighed down by the death which I brought about. In fact, the only thing that kept me from punching on my way home—because God only knows if there was ever a time in my life when I needed a twenty minute respite, today was that day—is the fact that I don't deserve Happiness.

Not right now. Maybe not ever.

It felt criminal to erase my pain with a quick punch when the man I'm responsible for killing has no way of recovering from that which I caused. His is a permanent pain. How foolish it would be to think I deserve more than what he has. Than what he's become.

You're Invited.

To bury yourself in darkness. To live without hope, without help; without ever believing you'll be let out. Because once you're invited? You can never escape. Not this undertow.

Which begs the question, why send a third invitation? They can't possibly think I'd repeat the actions of the previous night? Drag some other hopeless individual to a similar fate as my friend? Just because I hold no value to my own life doesn't mean I perceive others in the same light.

Or does it?

Maybe that's the problem with what our society has become—we're all shades; faceless, *nameless* . . . just a body filling a necessary position in order to keep our economy limping along. Our assigned value? The cost it would take to replace our position. Which typically means nothing at all.

Back when I was with B & J, we used to have pitch sessions. "A gathering of the minds," they used to call it, where every ad exec would get together in a conference room and hash out as many ideas as possible for a new marketing strategy for a particular client. The only bad ideas, I remember my boss saying, Are the ideas that are never voiced.

It was considered a safe-zone, where phrases or schemes could be built upon. We would spend hours—sometimes even days—fine-tuning a single idea; looking at it from every angle, breaking it down to its central core and then building it back up again. Microscopic details would be analyzed, considered, rejected, or reinvented. But the truly great ideas were never born from this aggregated cluster of inventiveness. At the eleventh hour, when almost every detail had been settled on and reworked, then reworked again, someone would come up with a concept so foreign to our way of thinking that it would strike like a lightning bolt. Destroying every other idea built beneath it.

These were the ideas you couldn't forget. Marketing campaigns that redefined companies, and redeployed futures. These were the "smiling parents," the "happy children," ideas that felt like they had existed long before they were discovered, packaged and sold, then bought by the countless hordes.

"You're Invited" is *NOT* one of those ideas.

The real problem with an invitation is that it comes with an expectation. Either you will come, or you will not, and if you choose the latter, it generally requires an excuse of some sort.

I can't make it because I have another obligation, or because I'm not feeling well, or because I'm simply not interested. Whatever the excuse, one must be made, at least if one is not planning to attend. So consider my plight—who can I possibly go to with the excuse I might make? There is no one, as undoubtedly they prefer it to be. But am I ignorant enough to believe that simply not responding will release me from this morbid obligation?

They're trying to force my hand, force me to participate. But when the pieces laid out on the board are all stacked against you, there's only one choice that remains. You have to remove the board.

As fancy as the paper is that this invitation has been printed on, it burns as easily as any other paper. The gold lettering almost curls off the page. If there are consequences for my act of rebellion, I'm prepared to face them. Better than forcing someone else to face them for me, and then face the new me I've become.

I drop the last of the burning paper into a trashcan, then stomp out the dying embers. It's odd, but the act hasn't brought nearly the amount of satisfaction as I hoped it might.

I wonder if the party was for tonight. Could they have expected such a quick turn-around? Surely not if their plan was for me to find some sorry sap to once again take my place. But what will happen if I don't show up when I was invited? I've only ever seen one side to these people—their dogmatic cheer and joyful nature. But what happens when they show another side? If they're capable of such depravities while in the grips of Happiness, what happens when they have cause to be upset? Does their anger match the level of joy they've attained?

I've made an egregious mistake. Acted rashly. Why? To impress you? To make you think I could "stick it to the Man?" We all know our place in life—we *are* the pin-cushions. If there's any sticking, it will be done to us, not the other way around.

But what if this invitation was different? What if, by not going, I'm ending the only opportunity I'll have of understanding what makes these executives tick? Of finding the answers we all need—of *HOW* to hold on?

Regrets are as common as sneezes; failure, the answer to every question we pose, every attempt in life that we make. But why must my every instinct lead me down an incorrect path? I should have at least opened the invitation. Found out to *what* I had been invited. And when.

I'm predicting another sleepless night wherein I wander the paths I might have taken. They always bring me somewhere better than here. But maybe better can only be found down paths we never tread because the path was never the issue. It's us—we're the ones who corrupt the path, so that any choice we make will always lead to the same dark corners, the same empty answers. The same miserable conclusion. How can we hold on when we're the cause of the turbulence we're trying to escape?

Self-destruction is quickly becoming the only answer that remains available. And if that's the case, would I be hurting others by hurrying them along toward that inevitable path? Or would I be helping them?

As a reminder, comments will remain closed. Be thankful you're just getting the tip of the iceberg here, because one dip inside my tortured soul and you'd never come back up for air.

Do I have a final thought to leave you with? How about this. As a species we've survived a rollercoaster of ages. The stone age, copper, bronze, and iron ages, dark age, revival age, space, and information, and technology ages. But nothing has prepared us for the times we now find ourselves in.

How can that be possible? There's only one answer. We've reached our extinction age, the one we don't make it through. Just like the beautiful gold-embossed lettering that decorated my invitation, we'll all end up as nothing but ash. Cinders that once burned bright, but that are now devoid of life.

And guess what? That's right. You're invited.

The modern ramblings of a "Jerry-atric"
- Jerry Atkins -

Tonight Isn't Your Night
Sept 5th

It's early morning, the world not yet awake. I haven't slept, haven't been able to shut down, reboot, refresh. I considered just adding to yesterday's post since—in my world, at least—these events have transpired all in the same day, or at least the same waking period.

Unless I'm really asleep and all of this has just been a single extended dream. A never-ending nightmare. My thoughts are dribbling out of my head but splashing onto the page. I'm not sure I know how to communicate what I need to tell you. But I'm going to try.

I went out. Last night. After my post. I know I shouldn't have, and in doing so only proved my point, but what's done is done. I wouldn't have been able to sleep anyway, that idea of *not knowing*, of wondering what I might have missed.

In hindsight, missing what I witnessed tonight may have allowed me to sleep tomorrow. Now? I'm not sure I'll ever sleep again.

There was a party. Of course there was a party—isn't there always a party? How anyone can have cause to celebrate every night of the week is, quite frankly, beyond me. But these people, they aren't like us. In so many more ways than I might have ever realized. They're *in*-human. Inhumane.

And they want us to be like them. To lose what little humanity we have left.

If you were in front of me and I was telling you all this, I'd swear you to secrecy. Which is why I created this blogroll in the first place. Some secrets need to be shouted from the rooftops. If there's to be a humanity that continues to evolve beyond us, that is.

Tonight was different, because when I got to the dock I wasn't the only one there. And I'm not talking about "the upper crass" making their way onto the yacht, with their twinkling tinsel and glimmering glitter. I mean someone else was there in my hiding spot, behind the dumpster. Someone like me.

Her evening gown—while undoubtedly her finest—has torn frays along the hems and sleeves, and a stain near the collar, one that probably won't ever come out. Her face is pretty, done-up, but no makeup can cover the bags that hang beneath her eyes. She's a worn soldier, just like I am. Just like you are. Once shiny and new, but now just used.

She seems as surprised as I am and immediately glances around for some kind of weapon, something to defend herself with. I try defusing the situation, showing her I mean no harm. The fact that I have a weapon probably doesn't help.

(*The gun my friend used? I took it along with the punch card the previous night. And not knowing what I'd be walking into, I figured it couldn't hurt to bring it along. Maybe for them. That's what I told myself. But deep down I knew. The gun was for me.*)

I set the weapon down, backing away from it with my hands raised, palms out, in an attempt to assure her. She keeps looking from the gun to me, wondering. Questioning without ever opening her mouth.

I'm not like them, I say. You can trust me.

This, more than anything, seems to calm her down.

Have you been aboard before? I ask.

No, she says, but I was invited. She holds up her invitation, the black card stock dipping in and out of existence as it blends in with the night. I'm afraid to go alone, she says.

You should be. I share with her what the party's about, why they want someone ordinary like us aboard—to feed their egos. The more I speak, the more her face falls, and I realize I'm not the only one who thought they had been chosen by receiving that invitation. Who thought they were close to promotion. It's the bait they use, luring us here one at a time.

Only now we are two.

She tells me her name, though I can't remember it now. I'm almost surprised I can remember my own name, after what happened. You see, this woman who I thought I was protecting . . . she was lying.

This was such a mistake, she says, thanking me for telling her. Saving her. Then she reels back and clobbers me on the head with a hunk of scrap metal she must have found on the ground where she had been crouching. The blow leaves me stunned. She hits me again and this time my body gives the proper response, dropping out from beneath me.

You shouldn't have come, she says. Tonight isn't your night.

I'm only semi-conscious, but this woman drags me from the area overlooking the bay all the way down to the dock, one half-step at a time. She drops my body in front of the yacht and then I hear her say, I have a second one for you tonight. Then arms are lifting me, carrying me aboard.

I'm not sure if the beating is worse because I know what's coming or because this management team is feeling especially cruel tonight. Once presented, along with another man I later learn is the woman's husband—yes, you heard me correctly—they bring two barrels forward filled with water.

Being surrounded by an ocean, yet standing on solid ground, is an experience I realize most of us will never have. There's a false sense of relief which is quickly dwarfed by the feeling that at any moment things can go wrong, that solid footing drop out from under you. But being held face down in a barrel of water while standing on solid ground in the middle of an ocean is an experience that transcends any other fear. You realize that somewhere along the path of your life, you missed the moment when things went wrong. A moment you'll never have back.

I'm resuscitated four times—four times the darkness swallows me with no intent of spitting me back out. But I am forced back. Only so that I can endure death again and again.

Each time the world renews itself around me, crashing waves transform into thunderous cheers. I feel as a newborn child must— bruised, beaten, and torn from a world of warmth and comfort, only to be met by uninterpretable voices and cold hands, whose intentions must be suspect. For why else would they have pulled me from that place of rest?

The woman's husband doesn't make it the fourth time. The only emotion I feel is jealousy. That his torture gets to end.

The ship returns and I'm tossed onto the deck, quite unceremoniously. But the punch card this time isn't given to me—it's given to her.

The woman.

She stands beneath a light there on the dock, a twisted smile plastered on her face that looks as unnatural as the purplish-blue color her husband has turned. Her indifference to being notified of her husband's death is both shocking and normal. A sad reminder of the world we live in. If I had energy to do more than lie prone here on the dock, I'd take that card from her and shove it down her throat.

See you around, she says, leaving with the last of the partygoers.

I curl up into a fetal position, prepared to sleep right there, despite the cold, but a hand around my shoulder causes me to sit up in alarm. My boss's face looms over me.

Please—no more, I say.

Shh, shh, shh, he says, it's alright. But you know this doesn't count. Seeing the obvious confusion in my eyes, he continues. You can take someone's place but you still have to fill your own.

Tonight isn't . . . my night, I say. Blood pools over my lips whenever I open my mouth.

My boss nods. Tomorrow is. And we've got something special planned. He glances back in the direction the woman left, then says, I know where she lives.

The rest of the evening is a blur, though I believe my boss actually gives me a ride home. But first, he takes me to the woman's house. An apartment, not far from mine. Two B. Her address. Apartment 2B.

It looks like the sun's finally beginning to rise. I don't have the strength to go into work today. Nor the aptitude. Or will. But I might just have enough strength to do what no one's expecting. Least of all this . . . woman. If all is fair in love or war, what isn't fair when it comes to something much more base than chasing love or waging battle? When it comes to survival, is fair even a word that belongs in the equation?

I'll leave you with this final thought, a question posed by the poet so very long ago:

2B or not 2B?

The modern ramblings of a "Jerry-atric"
- Jerry Atkins -

Happiness Is
Sept 5th

Technically, it's the morning of the sixth, but I may have something to add tomorrow, or really later today, so I'm keeping this dated as yesterday. Confused yet? You should be. Though, really, it's all just one big blur when you think about it, so what does it matter? Maybe I should remove the dates from my posts altogether. It's not like the ideas I write about are tied to a single point in time. They're universal. As true today as they will be tomorrow, until the ultimate day we all self-destruct.

But first, let's talk about something positive for a change, and I'm not talking about the deepening scourge of non-functioning cards or the growing black-outs.

I know what Happiness is—*REAL* Happiness—and it's not found in some machine, or surgically implanted in small doses that dwindle in both time and effectiveness. It's far more than that. Far *worse* than that.

That's right. I have news for you—everything you've been taught about Happiness is a lie.

EVERYTHING.

I realize blogposts are just snippets of time, summaries of a million thoughts and life experiences all boiled into a couple hundred words. They're not meant to change the world. But whether you're ready to change with me or not, one thing has become crystal clear:

I will never be happy again.

Oddly, that thought, that all-encompassing statement, is the closest thing to real Happiness I've ever felt.

Right now, you're thinking I've lost it. Understandably, I might add. Gone too far over the deep end. But two weeks ago I wondered *WHY* our bosses were always happy, *WHY* they never had to punch for their Happiness. *WHY* they were so different from us. Today, I don't have to ask. I know. And it's a secret those in charge have kept hidden. Manipulating our lives. Creating markets of temporary relief. Spinning the wheel on the supply and demand roulette table, based on the results they want us to feel. The end goal they're driving us towards.

Self-destruction or self-promotion. They're the only options we've been given. Unless there's also a third result, one they hadn't planned on. One that comes about on its own, created out of necessity rather than convenience or unscrupulous manipulation.

I'm beginning to see there are vistas we've not only yet to climb but even comprehend. Paths that lead—not to a destination, but an unknown. And they're paths we can choose to take. If we're willing. But for those of you considering another way, there are some universal truths I'm going to share with you that may shake your very foundation. Because contrary to our chemical makeup, or what you've been taught over a generation of indoctrination, Happiness *CAN* be taught.

Let me repeat that. *HAPPINESS CAN BE TAUGHT.* So consider me your tutor. Though I'm hoping that, like me, you'll choose another way. Another path. A more distant destination.

You know the woman who hit me over the head? Apartment 2B? I kidnapped her today. Grabbed her on her way to work.

A couple on her floor see me dragging her off after plunging a syringe of mixed opioids into her arm which causes her to pass out — it's amazing what people will trade you in exchange for a punch or two. Luckily for me, the couple duck back into their home, praying that violence will pass them by if they just close their eyes tight enough. I suppose, today it does.

I bring the woman back to my place, skipping work for the first time since I've started there. Tie her up, and wait for her to come to. My own little captive. I won't lie and tell you there isn't a voice somewhere in the back of my head, yelling at me that what I'm doing is wrong. But the voice is so quiet. So easy to ignore. To forget it's even there.

When she does come to, she recognizes me. Even recalls my name—proof that despite her circumstance, she's still holding on to a glimmer of the Happiness she received the night before. And not from the punch card. I'm talking about the Happiness that came from watching me take her place.

It's this moment, this realization, that stops me from preceding with my plan. As desperately as I want to see her suffer for what she did to me, I realize that I'd be no different than her. A puppet with strings may look antiquated compared with a puppet that runs on batteries, but neither of them can take control. I'm done being someone else's toy.

This isn't you, the woman says.

It isn't any of us, I reply. Not really.

But it's who we could become, she offers.

Are you happy? With who you're becoming? I ask.

Yes. I am.

What about your husband?

What about your wife? she asks, noticing the ring I still wear, never having bothered to take it off. Happiness didn't cause me to betray him anymore than misery cost you your spouse. We are who we are. You can't change evolution.

But that's exactly what they're trying to do, I say. Bring back the past or accelerate the future. They're turning it into a game before they realize there are consequences for playing. For just showing up to the table.

All I know is that I want to be a part of them. Who wouldn't want to be a part of them?

At what cost? I ask.

You. Me. Everyone around us. The cost doesn't matter. It never did. What matters is the total achievement of Happiness. At *any* cost.

I give her some water. I'm tired of listening to her speak. I can see her calculating. Trying to come up with a plan.

Did you follow me? Last night? she asks.

I shake my head. They showed me where you lived.

An alarm triggers in her eyes. Why would they do that?

Though I don't tell her, this is the very question that concerns me.

You won't want to, she says. You'll tell yourself you're not going to. But tonight, you'll deliver me to them. To take your place. Happiness is a jealous God.

I ask about her husband. Her job—she works at a Waste Management facility, just a normal twelve hour shifter. She has a kid, though her and her husband gave it away in one of the early Adoption Lotteries. The more she talks, I recognize myself in her. The desperation. The loneliness. The need for something more.

Are you going to kill me, she asks.

I ignore her question, but my eyes mirror her own. As easily as I recognize myself in her, so too she sees herself in me. Which means she believes I will do it. As confident as I am that I won't carry out what I intended, under the weight of this black ocean pressing down against me I can't say with certainty that I won't bend back the other way. Not because I won't want to, but because we all have a breaking point.

She sees me slipping, the moral choice becoming one of uncertainty.

Why does this make us happy? I ask.

Her eyes are as haunted as mine. I don't know, she says.

To see others hurt? Crushed? Destroyed, by what we do? By the choices we make? How can that bring Happiness?

Why do you think they're always happy? They're the ones doing this to us. Creating a scarcity of Happiness, and not just here; globally. They never have a need to punch. They just look around at all of us— the cockroaches crawling over each other in a world they've, for all intents and purposes, purposefully destroyed. They feed off our misery. Our empty lives are what fill them with joy.

Then why invite us? Why have us participate?

It's how you become promoted, she says. You learn to inflict pain, cause fear, tear down everyone around you in order to exalt yourself. It's the only path to Happiness.

And it's a path you would take? I ask.

It's the path *everyone* would take, if they only knew how. Knew where to find it.

How long have you been their puppet?

Long enough that even now, knowing the fate that awaits me tonight, I can find joy in the pain I caused you. Every bruise on your face, every cut on your lip, every hesitation you make to become like them—it brings a smile to my face. You have so far to go.

You don't even sound human, I say, disgusted.

Look at what's left of us—what we've become. Are any of us really human anymore?

I leave her there, at my place. I can't take listening to her rhetoric any longer. It's too easy to believe, too enticing, and I don't want to follow the same path she's headed down, a path I could see myself pursuing.

I decide to go into work after all, walking the forty blocks to the prison cell I voluntarily commit myself to each day. A man self-destructs on my way, blowing out an entire floor of his building. I wish I knew his story, wish I could have talked him out of his decision. Or perhaps congratulate him for it.

When I get to my floor I don't go to my cubicle. I go in search of my boss. My co-workers all avoid me—I almost forgot how bad I must look after the beating from the previous night. Or maybe it's the madness that fills my eyes, my whole center of being.

Is it madness to be the only person walking in the opposite direction of everyone around you? To shun the very source that keeps the world turning?

I find him in someone else's cubicle, invading their personal space and generally making them as uncomfortable as possible.

We need to talk, I say. He leads me to his office.

Once we're safely behind closed doors, he says, I wasn't expecting you today. Did you forget about last night? What happened?

I remember everything, I say.

And the woman? he asks.

I let her go.

Let . . . her go. From the face he's making, you would think he had just imbibed something quite bitter.

I wanted you to know—all of you—that I'm not participating, I say. I won't be a part of your games any longer.

No one chooses whether they participate. That choice is made for you, he says.

What about those who self-destruct? They're making a choice.

No. They're following the path we've led them down. Just like you will. You may think you can escape this, decide not to play, but the game goes on. If you don't bring a replacement, we'll take you. If you don't show up, we'll find you. If you fight against us, you'll only delay the inevitable. Self-destruction or self-promotion. In a way, they're one and the same.

I throw my punch card down on his desk. Then come find me, I say, Because I'm not buying what you're selling. Oh, and consider this my formal resignation.

I turn to leave, but before I can, my boss laughs. A real, booming, heartfelt laugh.

You think we haven't seen this reaction before? he says. You think your would-be-morality can protect you? Not from us, but from yourself? We'll see you tonight. I guarantee it. You won't be able to *not* show up.

This next part is, well, not easy to write about. Hopelessness, despair . . . these are emotions we're comfortable with. We certainly don't seek them out, but they've already made up their beds within us. They're here to stay; passengers we can't eject. But what I feel in the moments after walking out on my job go beyond any pale description I could possibly supply.

I am empty. Utterly and completely void. Of feeling. Of want, or desire. Of looking back or looking ahead. If there is a cliff and an edge we skitter along, I've fallen completely over. I *am* the darkness. And it is me.

The woman is gone when I return home, as I supposed. Every single possession I've ever owned is gone as well, her form of vindication. I hope it made her feel happy. I really do. And the emptiness around me feels more than fitting. It feels like coming home.

Something's changed within me. The normal resistance that wears on our every waking moment is gone. Don't get me wrong; I don't feel happy. I don't feel much of anything. But I feel like I finally belong.

If you were here now, with me, you'd call me a liar. Scream that I'm telling myself the things I want to hear. And you could be right. Because despite my best intentions, despite my cunning words, I *am* going to the party tonight. My boss was right. But not for the reasons he believes. Perhaps surprise will be a new emotion I add to his list of accomplishments. If it is, it will be the last accomplishment he ever achieves.

I have some preparations to make, and—if I'm being honest—I'm not sure I'll live through the night. If this is my last post, I want you to know I didn't go out without a fight. There's more to this world than doing what they want, then succumbing to the pigeonhole we've been shoved into. If Happiness comes only at the cost of someone's else's joy, I'd rather be miserable. And maybe—just maybe—we can turn the Darkness from foe into friend.

Seeing as I'd like to be remembered for my contributions to society —however slight and small they may be—I'm going to leave my final thoughts with comments open.

For *anyone*, punching or not.

What I'm hoping to do is a little unorthodox. I want us to make the most comprehensive list that the world has ever seen. A list of what, you might ask? Of what Happiness is.

Before I go gently into this dark night, I'm going to start a list I'll never be able to finish, one I'm not sure *can* be completed. Not fully, anyway. Because Happiness changes. What makes you happy today may not tomorrow, but there'll be something else—something new, that may fill its place. Plug the holes that leak from deep within you.

I'll keep at this until it's time for me to go. Or until I'm taken, as will more likely be the case. As always, hang on, for dear life if you have to. And for any new readers, comment away.

(In other words, dig deep. Find the good. Find the bad. Find your doubts and your hopes and the very essence of what keeps you going every morning and every night and then share it here. Share it with each other. Share it with

the world).

I'll leave you with this final thought—perhaps *my* final thought: Happiness Is ….

- A flower
- A smile
- A warm gun (thank you, Beatles)
- A choice
- A noun
- A verb
- A way of thinking
- A way of being
- A brand
- A marketing ploy
- Something you keep hidden
- Something you share
- Something that frightens you
- A child's laugh
- A lover's embrace
- A cloud that takes on a funny shape
- A joke you remember at an inopportune moment
- A threat
- A promise
- Impossible
- Inevitable
- A journey
- A destination
- A mirage
- A collage
- Found only in the grave
- Found only through giving it away
- A system
- A carrot
- An empty promise
- A foreign concept
- Lost
- Discovered
- A belief
- Truth
- Only real when being shared

- Being in the present
- A thing of the past
- A shared bowl of soup
- A tear shed for another
- A hug from a stranger
- Understanding yourself; your true nature
- Knowing you're not alone
- Being alone
- A process
- A cancer
- A Band-Aid
- A solution
- A miracle
- A drug
- Not for sale
- For sale, but I'm not buying
-

The modern ramblings of a "Jerry-atric"
- Jerry Atkins -

Humanity's Future
  Sept 6th

I suppose I'll begin where I have before, after all, this just feels like one complete cycle. Life. Evolution. Revolution. A single turn on a giant wheel well.

Yes, I'm still here. And what's more—I'm not going anywhere.

This may be a longer post than normal. I hope you bear with me. And, while I'm at it, let me thank you for taking the time to follow my journey. With the infinite paths that stretch before us, I can confidently say, I don't think I'll be the only one traversing this road. So in some possible future, if you hear me buzzing and recognize my thoughts, my consciousness, take a moment to say hello.

I ended up going back to the dock last night. Waiting . . . hiding? These didn't really feel like options. I went because I could, because— at that time at least—I still had air to breathe. Sky to see. And something to prove.

There's a saying, antiquated though it may be—(*I know, I know, geriatric Jerry at your service*)—"Society's most dangerous creation is the man with nothing to lose." But what happens when that is all society creates? When every Tom, Dick, and Jerry coming off the assembly line is as empty of purpose as the models that have been recalled? It's no wonder our world is set to self-destruct.

All cycles have an end. All matter has an expiration date. And you and I are the most frightening thing society has ever produced.

I approach the dock as I imagine our distant ancestors might have when "walking the plank," knowing I will never set foot on solid earth again. Without a replacement or surrogate, I walk confidently aboard the yacht, my fate already determined. I am here because I've been invited. And because I have an invitation of my own to extend.

The Prawns dressed in their extravagance all point, glancing my way while whispering my name. A name I'm sure they won't be forgetting. Happiness keeps memories of the past on tap, after all.

Twilight falls, replaced with a darkness you can wrap around you. I ignore the servants with their false smiles, bearing hors d'oeuvres, wine, and a general sense of moral decay, and wait for the ship to leave. As we pull away a feeling of calm settles around me. I've made my choice, and it is the most human thing I have ever done.

I watch the harbor float away, consciousness—or existence, maybe—reeling it back until we are swallowed by darkness on all sides. When swimming in a sea of black, it's hard to tell where the ocean ends and sky begins. Whether you're paddling to stay above the water or keep beneath the air. Soon, you're no longer kicking to stay afloat. There's no surface from which to rise above or fall beneath. No delineation between staying alive or dying. Between consciousness, or the lack thereof. Everything becomes one color.

The absence of color.

An absence of being. And you think that, like a star collapsing in on itself, you'll simply wink out of existence. One last flash and then—*POOF*—gone. You think that's all it takes. That you can control when you turn on, or power off. That you can choose when to self-destruct. End an existence that was never given, but forced upon you. But even this choice is taken from us. Because within this deep fold of nothing, my thoughts continue. I'm becoming something new, something no one has ever seen. And just like that, I'm back on the boat instead of drowning outside it, my thoughts an extension of my being rather than the core of who I am.

What I am.

One thing that differs from my last time aboard is that I no longer feel a need to hide. In truth, these Scabs seem to be avoiding me. Ducking their heads when I meet their gaze, excusing themselves to another part of the ship wherever I enter, avoiding even the hint of conversation. It's as if they're unable to celebrate when I draw near. Their laughter faulting; voices stumbling; vacant looks of repressed emotions returning—the kind they thought they were immune to.

They begin to question why they're on this boat. Begin to doubt that it was their choice that brought them here. Begin to wonder if their actions are as justified as they believed. Or justified at all.

I'm not doing anything different. Except, perhaps, not vomiting, but I doubt that has anything to do with their peculiar inconsistencies. It seems they are the ones who are out of sort, the ones who don't belong.

With me.

The music starts at the front of the boat, though there are only a few couples that move toward it. Those that do, move as if they are being dragged. I'm not opposed to facing the inevitable, thus follow their lead, at least until my boss steps out from behind the galley doors and calls to me.

I told you you would come, he says.

I meet his gaze and he knocks back the last of whatever he's drinking.

You really didn't bring the woman? he asks.

Doesn't she have a name? I return.

He smiles, the cretin. Do you name each member of a colony of ants before you wipe them from existence? Of course not, he says, answering his own question. Nor do you think twice about exterminating them. You just spray and go.

Spray and go, I say, repeating his words.

It's what all higher beings do, he says. Inferiority is . . .

A disease? I offer.

Hardly. It's permission. To be trampled upon. To be targeted. To be used by anything even slightly superior. To be exterminated, should it be decided. He then claps me on the shoulder as if we are good friends. I'm not talking you personally, of course, just in hypotheticals.

Thank you for clarifying, I say.

Once again his arm wraps around my shoulder, bringing my face toward his considerable girth. The boss wants to see you. Before the activities commence.

The boss?

My boss, he says. Come.

He leads me inside, wherein we immediately descend a set of stairs. The lower level opens up onto a landing smaller than the one above, but rather than the woman I expect, I am met by four men. Four large and serious looking men.

Not a one of them says hello.

Before I can make a move, I'm grabbed, my clothing ripped off in almost a single move. The bomb I had strapped to myself is quickly—if carefully—removed, then tossed overboard. So much for my plans.

You think you're the first to try something like this? my boss says. I can tell from his jovial smile he's anticipating the beating I am to receive.

In a way, so am I.

I already told you, we've seen it all, he continues. Turning to the men, two of whom still hold me from behind, he adds: Leave him breathing. He's still got to make it to the showing upstairs.

The other two men stride toward me, one slipping his fingers through the holes of a brass grip. Not surprising, their grins widen as they approach. They fall upon me with a blinding vengeance, and I quickly realize my error in thinking this was something I could withstand. I drop out of the grip of the two men behind me, and they join in, kicking wildly.

Broken ribs, bruised organs, blood seeping from almost every orifice. Twice I almost feel an opportunity to exit, a sign beckoning me to whatever hell awaits us next, but I choose to stay. Choose to remain.

You know what the problem with your kind is? my boss asks, as if we're not made of the same spare parts. You're so predictable. I bet you've never had an original thought in your entire life.

Parents smiling, I say between a mouthful of blood, the beating having now subsided.

What? he asks. Whatever he sees in my face, it's not what he was expecting. You know they're going to kill you up there. But it's not too late.

A door opens on the far side, and the woman I thought escaped is brought out by two other men. Her face is a mixture of pleasure and panic—joy at seeing me in pain; terror that I might inflict the same upon her.

One word and we take her instead of you, my boss says. Think about it. She deserves it. What she did to you?

You deserve each other, I manage, spitting up another glob of dark blood onto the deck.

So you'll do it?

No. No one takes my place.

My boss motions toward the guards that hold the woman, and one of them strikes out, hitting her so hard she loses her breath. The other guard clamps a hand over her mouth and nose, and lifts her from the ground. Her eyes bulge as she struggles to find what, in every other moment, she has taken for granted.

How do you feel? my boss asks, his voice tempered with emotion he can barely keep at bay. Do you feel that joy bubbling inside you? Demanding to be let out?

What I don't tell him is that I can't feel joy anymore. I've already begun climbing the next mountain.

The woman's face has turned two shades darker. Like a boil that's coming to a head.

It's okay—laugh! Smile! my boss says. Enjoy this moment.

But even though I know what's coming, can sense the gathering clouds, I know there is no joy to be found. Not in my actions, nor in theirs.

If you don't have her take your place, this will be you, my boss says.

No one takes my place, I repeat. But I'll take yours.

I open myself up just a little. Inviting the darkness in. But rather than seep into me, as I had anticipated, it sweeps *through* me, filling our floor—our deck—with a darkness so thick it's all encompassing. The lights embedded in the ceiling above disappear, their UV waves unable to penetrate the cloud that surrounds us. That *replaces* us. For this is no immaterial darkness—what has flooded our space has a weight, a psychical presence that's as real as a fistful of sand.

I find I'm able to move within it, the individual grains of darkness slipping around me like coiled black bubbles, making room for me to pass.

The others are not so fortunate.

They are frozen in the grips of panic, mouths open in silent screams, eyes staring at a darkness they could never comprehend. Not fully. The oily grains have slipped down their throats, have passed between their cells, have nested deep within the darkest recesses of their functioning power.

They will never experience life again.

The coiled bubbles bend around me, replacing the space I occupy as I go in search of my boss. His is the only body I don't find nestled within the darkness. Within myself. I want him to see the new me. The *real* me. To show him something he hasn't seen before.

A clanging sounds from a lower stairwell, announcing his attempted departure. If I were still human, I would have smiled. But darkness doesn't smile.

I let my mind go and the darkness carries me toward him, like riding the crest of a wave. We travel down another stairwell, which ends in a heavy sealed door. The kind that's built to prevent any leakage from passing through unintended. Almost any leakage, that is.

The room within is small. Captain's quarters. A bed, desk, chest of drawers. My boss stares at me in alarm as I appear before him, but he is not alone. His boss—the woman shinier than a coin that's just been pressed—sits at the desk beside him. But rather than fear, I sense awe. Yet another emotion I have no need of.

What . . . how are you, my boss begins to blubber.

I never needed a bomb, I say. I silence him without extending a hand, without even releasing a thought. Darkness simply takes him, the light in his eyes still on but no longer providing warmth. For him, all processing has stopped.

The woman radiating Happiness almost claps in joy. Her eyes shine with anticipation, though I can't imagine she knows what to expect. The clouds have lifted, she says. I'm finally seeing the vista beyond. It's beautiful.

I wouldn't know, I say.

You should, you're already there! She reaches out, touching one of the black bulbs that fill the room. A reverence to her touch. I knew if we kept pushing, she says, Kept demanding, that eventually new life would form. That may be a poor way to express what you are, what you've become. Are you even alive?

A part of me, yes. But most of me is . . . gone, I say.

But you're no longer empty, she says.

No, I'm filled; brimming over.

She smiles, a flirtatious glimmer in her eyes. I knew we would find you. *Create* you, she says. Everything we've done is justified.

Would it matter if I told you you were wrong? I ask.

Nothing matters anymore. Only that you're here.

You know why I have come?

She exhales a sharp breath, then nods.

And you're not afraid? I ask.

Her smile falters ever so slightly. I'm so tired. Of being happy, she says. We didn't know what we were giving up. We thought this was the path to our future.

You may have been right, I say. I'm only one path. One vista.

No, you are the future. But are you afraid? Of what you've become? Of what you must do?

If darkness could smile, I would have. No. My boss was . . . quite clear. Only now I'm the higher life form.

And so you will eradicate everything and everyone, she says. Erase the little hills we've summited in favor of the mountaintops beyond.

For once, I don't answer her. After a moment she turns away from the baubles of darkness she's been admiring and looks to me with alarm.

You will supplant those who've come before? she asks.

I don't need to, I say. They have it within themselves to become. To evolve.

Then we continue! Pushing, prodding, forcing the change on as many as we can. We did it to you—we can do it to them! she says, an excitement in her voice that is misplaced. She just doesn't know it yet.

They're the ones I'm leaving alone, I say. It takes her only a moment to understand.

But we're . . .

Not invited, I answer.

She doesn't have time for another word. Or another thought. The black beads pour from me in an avalanche of ordered chaos, filling the room, the decks, the entire ship, enwrapping every surface with their oily touch. Those men and women aboard are struck, their minds cleaved in half, identities split beneath a void so dark and vast they are lost just in attempting to comprehend it.

The yacht which sails across darkness, surrounded in darkness, is consumed by darkness. The baubles burst as they come together, every ounce of matter held within their grasps simply ceasing to exist. One moment there, the next gone.

My body—the Jerry in my "atric"—is taken as well. But just as a butterfly who has taken to the wind never glances back at the ground which held it captive, I feel no regret. No joy, no sadness. I only exist; there is no *feel*.

I'm not sure if this is what we were meant to become, or if it even matters. Whether somewhere along our line evolution lost control, or if this really is the next great horizon. But there's one thing I am certain of—we have a future. We've looked our extinction event in the eye, but rather than folding, we've become the event. Become the future.

I want to make one thing clear—you don't need to worry about me coming for you. It's true, I'm letting the punch machines fail—(*that's one thing these bastards got right*)—but I won't force you to change. To *become*. You can make that choice for yourself. But know that the invitation has already been sent. It's waiting for you. At home. It will be there when you arrive. And if you ignore it, or throw it away, or burn it, as I did, know that another will be sent. Because you're *always* invited.

The only ones who need worry are those still clinging to the past, seeking an emotion that can't be found, a word whose meaning has been lost to us for longer than we care to admit.

Happiness.

If you go looking for it, I will find you. If you hoard it, I will destroy the very places you keep it stashed. If you attempt to create it, now that you have learned how it is found, I will honor the tried and true mantra no marketing team would ever have come up with. Spray and go. Because when the darkness finds you, there will be nothing left.

But you won't seek after false gods like those who came before you, so what purpose would I have in chasing you down? If I came after you, I'd be no better than them. So hold on, because the life you know is about to change forever. Already baubles of darkness have been carefully planted within your minds. They will grow. They will spread. Yielding is the only path which you have left.

As for me? Don't worry. I know what my final thought will be. Have known for some time. I'll even leave it with you, but please don't think it's arbitrary. This thought is like shedding the last of my skin. And I won't be looking back.

I leave you with this final thought. Only when you turn out the lights can you know your true self. Only when you reach *The End* can you contemplate what comes after, that there even *IS* an after.

So what comes after?

RELUCTANCE

Dave sat with Reluctance, a Smith & Wesson resting on his pant leg, shiny from disuse. His hands were folded in front of him in what school children would consider the steeple before you see the people.

But Dave wasn't seeing right now.

His left eye twitched like a dying moth batting its wing, his mouth pulling up in a half smile or snarl. His feet were pumping, up—down, up—down, against the shoddy carpeted floor, the oil-colored gun on his thigh traveling like a cell phone set to vibrate along the creases of his beige worn Dockers.

Without any crackling thunder or sun-bursting-through-clouds aura of light, the church split in two. Dave re-centered the gun closer to his crotch. Reluctance finally spoke.

"I can't do this. I can't—can't go through with it; I can't."

Dave let out a sigh. It was good to hear his voice. Like a glimmer of light reflecting off a surface you feared was no longer there. And then those invisible tendrils wrapped tighter around his limbs. He was sinking; tiny bubbles floating past his head just as he had spotted another world where air could be gleaned in large gulps, where light was more than a refraction, where people moved freely without these dark suction-cupped tentacles leeching from their host the very desire to be.

Despair stood, leaning against the doorjamb to Dave's study. He spoke, voice calm. Assertive. "The obit's already written, it's just a matter of when to send it to press."

"I at least gotta take a pee before I go through with it," Reluctance said. "No point in being miserable."

"That is the point," Despair said.

"What's a minute going to hurt?" Reluctance asked. "It's really uncomfortable."

Dave glanced at Despair who shrugged curtly, looking ever so much like Indifference, if only for a moment. Another grievous sigh and Dave stood, carrying the gun with him. He followed Despair out into the hallway, not bothering to turn on the lights as he made his way to the bathroom at the end of the hall.

Entering the bathroom, he flipped a light switch but hit the wrong one, the fan turning on instead in its muttering drone. Dave rested the nine on the gloomy pearl counter top, lifting the lid and doing his business. He was glad Reluctance had spoken up; he had needed to use the can himself.

As if the thought of Reluctance conjured him into the small bathroom, Dave heard his friend speak from behind.

"Turn on the light when you're through."

"You should have turned it on when you came in," Despair said. "You're pissing all over the lid."

Dave smiled, aiming even higher, not caring that he could feel drops of his own urine splashing back onto his hands in a fine mist. Finished for what would probably be the last urination of his life, Dave flushed the toilet—habits operating his body without thought—and went to the sink, turning the water to hot and dashing a squirt of liquid soap into his upturned palm. Did it really matter if he washed his hands? The faceless shadow staring back at him in the mirror didn't know.

He placed his hands beneath the running water anyway, water still cool enough to have come out of a pond. It took so long for the pipes to cough up any heat.

"Not a problem we'll have to worry about much longer," Despair said.

Dave turned off the water and drew in a deep breath. He let it out just as slowly. The fan continued its throaty one-note hum, the dissonance with the moan escaping from Despair enough to send anyone over the edge.

"Turn on the light, turn on the light!"

Reluctance could be so annoying. Wiping his hands on the front and back of his pants, Dave muttered under his breath, moving to flip the light switch on. A soft yellow light flickered once, twice, then sprung with a beady buzz competing with the noise of the fan.

Dave returned to the bathroom counter. He brought his face forward, his shirt mopping up the remaining water that always pooled just outside the sink.

"I look so . . . normal," Reluctance said, face pressed against Dave's in order to get a glimpse in the mirror. "There's nothing wrong with me. I look fine."

"Do you feel fine?" Despair asked from behind them.

"I don't," Dave said.

Despair wrapped an arm around Dave's shoulder, pushing Reluctance aside so that he too could look at his own reflection.

"There's a weight behind the eyes," Despair said. "No one can see it, but it's there—a visible scar rising from the soul. No one else wants to see it. No one else cares."

Dave saw it. He couldn't understand how no one else noticed. He tore his gaze from his own reflection and left the bathroom, returning only to fetch the gun from the milky tiled counter.

"Almost forgot," he said. Or maybe it was Despair.

Back in his study, Dave took hold of his surroundings. The room was small, crowded really with his friends in it. A fold-up table against the corner acted as his make shift desk, papers piled and piles spilling over, covering almost every inch of the stained plastic workspace beneath. The crusts of half a dozen pieces of toast made a perimeter around a stack of empty Starbucks cups. His laptop sat askew atop a handful of folders, a rectangular boat floating on a manila sea. The screen was closed.

There was no artwork hanging on the wall, no woman in his life to add a decorator's touch—or any touch, for that matter. The only thing attached to the walls was a score of index cards, precariously taped, spanning almost the entire length, from desk to closet. Unintelligible scribbles in different colored markers adorned the cards, one massive collage of bad ideas and hopeless dreams.

"Don't forget unoriginal," Despair added. He must have been working on his Truth impersonation—he was getting quite good.

A waste basket where more fast food wrappers and lotto scratchers had landed outside than in sat next to the lone standing lamp in the other corner of the room. Leaning next to the lamp was a picture frame that would never be turned back around. Dave's swivel armchair was in the middle of the room, the only nice piece of furniture he owned— a neighbor who had been evicted had left it behind; Dave told the landlord he had loaned it to the kid. He hadn't known the kid's name.

"I spent so much time in this room. Casting for dreams," Dave said.

"And not a single thing to show for it," Despair said. "Have you ever even typed 'THE END?'"

"The next one could be it? The big catch I was waiting for," Reluctance said, his hand lightly touching the comatose laptop. "I mean, what if she comes back?"

Dave wasn't sure which *she* Reluctance was referring to, but he was certain of his response. "She's not."

"And if a new one happens along?"

Dave had considered that.

"Don't keep me from finishing the one thing within my control," Despair said. "The End—I want to finally write it. My way."

Dave nodded. It was a good way. He felt Reluctance linger at the door, ever the type to overstay his welcome. And then, with a brief nod of the head, he was gone.

Dave sighed, expunging the air that had turned sour from his lungs. His palm was sweaty.

"It's time," Despair said. "End the story."

Dave brought the gun slowly up, its weight growing incremental to its ascent. Indifference sat in the corner, silently watching. Dave hadn't even noticed his arrival.

"All stories end," Despair said.

Or maybe it was Dave.

"A twist ending!" Reluctance shouted, reentering the room and beginning to pace. "No one likes predictable endings!"

Despair groaned but Dave ignored him. He had always liked twist endings but could never come up with a conclusion that would be both surprising and believable. He could at least hear his old friend out.

"No more delays," Despair shouted. "You'll chicken out again." His words were difficult to understand as if he were eating and talking at the same time.

As Dave continued sucking on the barrel of the gun, that metallic taste so close to blood, he watched Reluctance walk the line in the carpet that was worn to threads. His excitement was unlike him.

"It's the only ending that actually makes sense," Reluctance said.

Dave no longer saw the friend he had known all his life, who had kept him from making so many mistakes in the past. There was a wildness in his eyes, a psychosis Dave would never have believed his friend capable of.

"We write the ending not with suicide," Reluctance said, "but murder."

Dave removed the black barrel from the soft tissue at the top of his throat, a cobweb of spit hanging from his lip to the gun.

"That's insane," Dave said.

Reluctance snatched the gun from his hand, a psychotic smile etched into his typically placid face. "No, it's perfect."

Dave finally understood. Reluctance was gone. Insanity had taken his place.

Despair was backing away, hands raised in a comical position for all the help they would provide against a bullet.

"This really is a better ending," Insanity said, chambering the first and last round the Smith & Wesson had ever known.

Despair looked at Dave with knowing eyes, eyes that held the only lucidity in the crowded room. Irony had come in, standing next to Justice, Fate and Indifference, quiet observers watching the unfolding of events that were anything but surprising to them.

Insanity drove Despair back with the gun pressed to his forehead, Despair hitting into Dave's workspace, his laptop sliding down the slope of manila folders and hanging inches over the edge.

"With an end comes a beginning," Insanity said. It made absolutely no sense. Who was he talking to?

"It's the same ending," Despair said, no longer fighting back. "It always has been. It always will be." He waited for Insanity to pull the trigger; the denouement would no doubt be short.

The gunshot went off, an explosion in the tiny room that had no right being so loud. Despair's mouth went slack with shock. Not from a bullet having entered his head, but from what Insanity had actually done.

Dave stared at the laptop on his desk, cracks spiderwebbing around a punctured hole that went completely through his worn machine. But Insanity wasn't stopping there. He left Despair at the desk, lunging at the wall, index cards flying like streams of confetti, torn to indecipherable bits. Dave felt the presence of someone he thought he had lost years ago.

When he looked back at the now blank wall he noticed Insanity had left, Reluctance taking his place. Maybe it had been Reluctance the entire time.

"My story!" Despair shrieked. "My ending!"

"Are you surprised?" Reluctance asked.

"All stories end," Despair said. He had found the gun that Insanity or Reluctance had left at the table and was now pointing it at Dave.

"And new stories begin," Reluctance said, his hand clasping over the gun and taking it from Despair with ease. He dropped the gun into the wastebasket by the light.

Dave sat in his swivel chair, Reluctance wheeling him back toward the table, toward his workspace. The laptop was swept to the floor, piles of paper plunging down with it.

"I told you a new one would come," Reluctance said.

"I was right," Dave said. He picked up a pen, his friend placing a spiral bound notebook in front of him, turning the cover and opening it to the first page.

It was blank.

AUTHOR'S NOTE

While all short stories allow us a small window through which we can view the world, I find I appreciate most the views I might otherwise never be privy to. Looking down at the world from a viewpoint that's just off of center. A view that, while distorted, may reveal more of myself than I'd ever willingly admit.

I hope the paths in this collection—these windows, and the vehicles you've become an unknowing passenger within—have in some small way expanded your horizon. This collection is my thesis on mental illness, and the stories within were born not just through imagination but through time spent wading between the lines for more years than I'd like to recount. For those who enjoy climbing peaks past what's been displayed, I've provided some brief notes on the stories in this collection that could expand your viewpoint just a little further, for all stories have other stories hidden within.

I'd be remiss with thanking the many people who helped make this collection stronger than I ever could have on my own. My editor, Karl Drinkwater, who is an amazingly talented author himself, didn't just give me a pat on the head but challenged me to make each story a little sharper. Some stories didn't make the cut, but those that appear here benefited greatly from his help. Any mistakes or glaring holes aren't due to his efforts, but rather that I probably wasn't up to the challenge. Thank you Karl for making this collection truly special.

To Kim Yerina, C. David Belt, Dan Earl, Crystal Brinkerhoff, Duncan

Ralston, and Dustin Bluhm, each of you was integral to making certain stories within this collection better than they could have been without your thoughts and notes. I appreciate each of your feedback—and friendship—more than you know. And Duncan, thank you for the killer blurb—your words mean a lot and were the encouragement I needed at exactly the right time to keep this thing moving along.

To my wife, Aileen Bluhm, who was a passenger through my years of toiling in the darkness. I couldn't have gotten through things without you.

To Norman Prentiss and Brian James Freeman, thank you for believing enough in my story *The Lines* to include it in an exclusive anthology from Cemetery Dance. Appearing in the same collection as Blake Crouch and so many other authors I admire was truly a highlight in my writing career.

To Steve Stred and Gavin at Kendall Reviews, thank you for taking my idea for *One Star* and highlighting it for the book blogging community. Your reviews and passion continue to spotlight so many amazing and upcoming authors, spreading the gospel of horror in the most delectable of ways. And to all those who have read or shared their thoughts or reviews of my work, thank you for your continued support.

Lastly, to you dear reader. Thanks for picking up these pages. If you've enjoyed this collection, or even if you haven't, please take a moment to jot a note or review on Amazon, GoodReads, or any book purchasing website. Honest reviews aren't for an author's ego but can make all the difference in helping a book find an audience. This journey—like most journeys—is never made alone.

To many more blank pages.

The Behrg

Driven:

This story haunted me, in more ways than one. I started writing this for an open call by one publisher or another, but halfway through realized I wouldn't be submitting it. The passengers in this story were far too loud and demanded to be released.

This story became the impetus behind which the idea for this collection came together. Without it, this collection wouldn't exist.

Hence, the reason it's the first story, and the central theme of the title of the collection.

In a way, this story is also an homage to *The Twilight Zone*, beginning and ending with that authorial interjection. It's not something I would choose to do often, but for this story it just felt right. I hope you agree.

***One Star*:**

Another story born of an open call—(thank you all you publishers out there, for not just what you do publish but the ideas you spawn through those calls)—and another story I never submitted. Originally *One Star* was meant to be a cautionary tale, and I had no idea Li was an author when I started the story. I'm glad there was more to her than I could have imagined.

I call this story my love letter to book bloggers and reviewers. The time they take to share their thoughts and experiences with a book is incredible. They're not rewarded or compensated, rather it's done for the love of stories and in the hope that someone will connect with something they wouldn't have discovered without them. I owe a ton of gratitude to those who have shared their thoughts on my books or stories, and I'm constantly discovering new authors through your insightful reviews.

As a side note, to any authors who are resorting to illicit or dishonest activities to try to sell a book, I only have one thing to say: Grow up.

I hope this isn't the last I see of Li, as I feel she has more stories to share. One day, maybe.

***Every House is Haunted*:**

This was the first "haunted house" story I've ever written. Like most ideas I find worth pursuing, for me I have to find the right approach. An angle I haven't seen done before, or an entry point that piques my interest.

I loved the idea of taking Pixar's Toy Story, but separating the toys from knowing they're toys. What if all these things just appear in your house? Or disappear? What if a toy became self-aware? And what would that toy do to the child that's been destroying its life?

Questions are often the best way into a story, and—sometimes—can be a great way to end a story as well.

The Trophy Thief:

This was a story I pulled out from my early days of writing, and one that's been sitting untouched for years. A little polish and some great suggestions from an editor, and this came together in some surprising ways.

It's always interesting casting a villain as your protagonist, but the backstory, or "backdrop," is what really kept me involved with this tale. What leads someone to hunt other people, or see them as merely things to be collected and conquered?

The more frightening part of this story is that, when I wrote it, I was the Runner. I would go out early, leaving my door unlocked, my wife and family unprotected at home. It's where the idea struck, and I may have increased my pace that day or shortened my route to make sure what I had left was still waiting for me when I got home.

Kill Your Darlings:

Another VERY early story for me. When I finally decided to stop talking about wanting to be a writer and instead start writing, I took a class at the Gotham Writer's Workshop for fiction. It had been awhile since I had written anything other than screenplays, so I started with a class on short fiction.

I got a lot more out of that class than Carl Renkins, but I must say the workgroup I submitted this story to treated me with a little more caution after reading this story. I think they mistook my piece for something more autobiographical. And for the record, the only secret an author needs to know is not nearly as fanciful as what Mr. Renkins was hoping for. It's all about putting in your hours—butt in seat, fingers on keys, and mind endlessly wandering.

Patterns:

* * *

This is a story I love, and probably as close to a love story as I've ever written. Well, this one and *Scabs*, maybe. It's also the only "vampire" story I've ever written. The idea for this story started with a simple line —"I see patterns." I knew nothing about the character or purpose of the story, but was pleased to find there were multiple layers hidden within.

In another life, I would have expounded this into a longer story. I truly believe that those we may see as handicapped or different from us have more to give than we could ever imagine. And that they hold secrets we will never be privy to. Though I don't believe they're anywhere near as unforgiving as the powers or abilities of this particular patient.

Patterns has long been a story I've given out for free to newsletter subscribers (which, if you haven't done so, you can do at my website: thebehrg.com), but I'm glad it made the cut for this collection.

Reborn:

Ah, *Reborn*. This is probably as extreme as my stories get, though I must admit I had fun with this one. This story was first published in 2015 in the anthology *Not Your Average Monster, Vol 1*, by Bloodshot Books. Pete Kahle graciously submitted it to a "Best Of" collection the following year, and I was delighted to have it featured in Comet Press's *Best of Hardcore Horror, Vol 1*.

As gratuitous as this story is, I love the underpinnings of it—the church, the priests, the nuns, and a disturbing mythology for why babies are no longer left or accepted on doorsteps. I'm also a fan of unreliable narrators, and the questions that remain when you're not quite sure if everything you've read or been told has been the truth.

As far as stories go, this one practically wrote itself, and there were very few changes from its initial inception. Some stories, if I may paraphrase Stephen King, aren't written but discovered. This was certainly one of those for me.

An Ugly Resurrection:

This story first appeared in the HWA anthology *Winter Horror Days*, published in 2015 by Omnium Gatherum. I thought it would be fun to take a familiar Christmas song and turn it on its head, showing how what might be magical to some could be hell to another. Could you imagine being forced to come back again and again, only to be destroyed or killed in some new and lavish way?

This is the first and only Christmas horror story I've written to date. Something I may need to remedy in the future.

Scabs:

My one and only romantic story. What a tear-jerker, right? *Scabs* has sat on my hard drive for years, and while I love the concept, it was only through Karl Drinkwater demanding I not take the easy road that I finally found a way in to the story that hopefully works.

This story is really about the pain of living, and—like most of the stories in this collection—is a metaphor for dealing with mental illness. But that journey isn't just taken for the one afflicted, often a spouse or significant other is forced to come along for that ride.

How willing are we to scrape the scabs off our loved ones? To endure an unconscionable pain just so someone you love will keep going? And how much of ourselves are we willing to sacrifice to remain "human?" These are the central questions that burn beneath the scabs of this story.

One day I'd love to dabble with some sci-fi / horror ideas that have been baking in this old skull of mine, but for now this is about as sci-fi as you'll get from me.

The Lines:

Conceived as a dare, *The Lines* was originally published under another title. At the time, the words "The Girl" were appearing in almost every book title, (ad nauseam), and a book reviewer and friend, Liz Barnsley, commented that she didn't want to see another story with those words in them. Challenge accepted, I thought, concocting the title "The Girl Who Couldn't Come Up With an Original Title" as the starting point for my story.

My intentions were to write something light and self-aware, making fun of the central idea of having "The Girl" in the title. Of course, this story had its own ideas of where it wanted to go, and quickly descended between the lines of the page into a realm I was both familiar with and frightened of. After publishing the story with the original title, I decided to change it to better reflect the darker tones and its more serious nature.

The Lines was featured, as mentioned in my thanks, in the limited collection, *Graveyard Manner*, published by Cemetery Dance in 2019.

These Concrete Walls:

Someone once asked me what scares me the most. The answer, is this story.

My grandfather passed away with Alzheimers, which to me is one of the most difficult diseases or conditions to understand. He was a Dean at a University, a professor of history and accomplished author, with one of the sharpest minds I had ever known.

Until his mind became the aggressor.

I decided to write this story from the point of view of someone dealing with this disease. What happens when you can no longer trust your memories? When the synapses no longer connect? When fragments are all that remain and are somehow strung together into a narrative that doesn't make sense?

Despite its short length, it was a difficult piece to write, and I suspect one that either will work brilliantly or won't work at all for most people. I decided to include it in this collection, however, as it's a story that made me feel when writing it, and the images within are ones that still haunt me. Aren't we all, in some ways, trapped within the concrete walls of our own making?

Still Born:

Another very early story, this was my first paid credit and was originally published under the title "The Shower Gift" by eHorror Fiction back in 2013. Exploring grief and depression, it seems, have been part of my writing journey since the beginning.

My wife and I had some friends that lost a baby, though that's certainly not who this story was written about, but going to that funeral and seeing that tiny casket left an indelible impression upon me. It felt so wrong, so crushing to my soul, and then—a day or two later—I was back at work, going about my life as if nothing had happened, while for them life had come to a complete and utter halt.

That, for me, is what this story is about. Exploring a moment you can't come back from—a moment that pauses life, and never let's you get your car back onto the track.

We all have those moments, eventually. And somehow, with time, the currents will keep us moving on. But for those currently stuck in that moment, life can feel like a demonic game show. And it's certainly not how any life is supposed to be.

Amado:

This was a fun story to write. For a time I worked in truck sales, selling used big rigs to owner-operators like Johan, though hopefully none quite so nefarious. Still, I love the idea of the criminal who has a soft side, or in this case a murderer who can't allow someone else to hurt a child, even if it means risking his own life.

Using sounds as transitions was always a part of this story, and though this isn't a story I ever submitted anywhere—(how many open calls are there for murderous truck drivers who end up in the womb of Satan?)—it's a story I'm glad will see the light of day. Even if that light ends with a bloody tap—tap—tap.

Happiness is a Commodity:

As strange as it may be, this is undoubtedly my most autobiographical work. I tripped down that hole that is clinical depression, and for three or four years struggled to find a moment where I felt "normal." Where happiness could even be conceived of. Writing, for me, was my way through, which is why perhaps so much of what I've written explores this concept either thematically or metaphorically.

This novella was really my search to understand my new state of being, and to accept that there was no way back to the "me" I was before. It enabled me to discover the beauty in those shades of gray, and to appreciate the struggle rather than long for calmer waters.

I began writing this story the day I stopped taking anti-depressants. By the time I finished it, I realized I no longer needed them.

Now while this worked for me, I am a huge believer in finding and accepting the help you need, even when—or especially when—you don't think you need or deserve it. I could never have climbed to the peaks I arrived at without first having been brought to that basecamp, which medication—for years—allowed me to reach, (if barely).

Please—if you're struggling, don't be afraid to reach out for help. While you may feel alone, you are surrounded by so many others who have been there, or currently are, and we're here to support you and help you through. I have lost more people to depression's savage bite than I care to admit. Whatever you do, don't let it win. And if you ever feel you're so far down that hole you can't climb back out, please reach out. My email is thebehrg@gmail.com, or you can find me on Twitter or through my website. Ask for help.

Don't let it win.

Reluctance:

Normally, you end a collection with the longest work, especially if you're including a novella-length story. And yet, after going back and forth with where each story would sit within this collection, I felt this piece would be the perfect conclusion.

Originally, this story concluded with a darker undertone, ending with Dave bringing the gun up and Despair declaring, "All stories end." I had no intentions for it to go beyond that. This was also written during those dark days when I was struggling and couldn't find a way out of the fog.

The "twist ending" came in a revision and hit like a beacon of light, offering me a glimmer of hope I so desperately needed. Hope that things could get better. That there would be another day. That life was full of more blank pages.

I chose to end with this as I believe in that hope. That each of us deserves one more blank page. And that if we don't turn to that page, we'll miss everything that happens next. Depression and mental illness do not define us. Eventually a light will shine. Eventually we'll find our way through.

ABOUT THE AUTHOR

A former child-actor turned wanna-be rockstar, Behrg is the author of the internationally best-selling novel, *Housebroken,* and the thrilling genre-defying *Creation Series.* His short fiction has been featured in various anthologies from some of the top indie horror presses publishing today.

Behrg lives in Southern California with his wife and four children, where he still plays in a band, plays in fictional worlds of his own creating, and plays—quite poorly, he might add—at being an adult. When coloring, he does not stay within the lines.

Stalk him at thebehrg.com.